Beyond
SOMNIARE

AVA WIXX

First Edition: November 2024
Published in the United States of America by
Wicked Wixx Press.
The Wicked Wixx Press Logo is a trademark of
Wicked Wixx Press.
Originally published under the title
Somniare: October 2016

Cover Art, Ava Wixx Logo, Wicked Wixx Logo, & Interior Book
Graphics by Lindsay Tiry of LT Arts
Illustrations by J.N. Sheats
Edited by Melissa Ringsted of There For You Editing

Print ISBN: 978-1-955950-39-8
Kindle ISBN: 978-1-955950-40-4
EPUB ISBN: 978-1-955950-41-1

For more information visit: avawixx.com

Deep into that darkness peering,
long I stood there, wondering,
fearing, doubting, dreaming
dreams no mortal ever
dared to dream before.
~Edgar Allan Poe

FREE! FREE. FREE?
NO LONGER LOST IN DREAMS,
SHE IS NOW TRAPPED IN REALITY ...

Chapter 1

"I can't. I can't do it." I gripped a scalpel in my right hand, my left arm wound tightly around my abdomen, blood seeping into my dress. My fingers trembled, partly from cold, the rest from nerves.

I was dying … again.

"I told you, I want you to." Miles' dark eyes beseeched me, as if I was doing something for him, and not the other way around. But he looked so fragile in his hospital bed, his face gaunt and drawn, his muscles atrophied. None of that mattered, though—he was alive … very much alive. I couldn't take that from him. Not now. Not after everything he'd already suffered. *If only I hadn't gotten to know him at all.*

"I-I can't." The scalpel slipped from my grasp, clattering to the floor. My knees wobbled and my vision danced just as I staggered into Miles' bed, slumping against the scratchy sheets. I inhaled a ragged breath, the scent of bleach and blood assaulting my nose.

"Remy!" Miles' arms slid around me. He grunted in an attempt to lift me, but I sagged against him, complete dead weight.

This is it. After everything. I'm really going to die all the way. I had so many regrets. Lost opportunities and things I'd never get to experience. The list was too long to even begin contemplating.

I don't wanna die.

Every molecule in my body screamed out for self-preservation. And yet something had been altered in me while I was in Somniare. I used to only care about Makoto and myself, playing in the grey areas of moral ambiguity, but now I cared about more. It made me feel lighter somehow, even as my consciousness was dragged into the murky depths of death.

The steady cadence of Miles' heart monitor permeated my waning consciousness, causing me to idly wonder why no nurses or doctors had shown up yet. He'd been in a coma for who knew how long. Wasn't a patient like him waking up cause for some kind of attention? But I'd never been in a human hospital before, so what did I know beyond what I'd seen on TV and in movies?

"Re-ems." Makoto's multi-layered fox voice shifted to his deep original male tone in the middle of saying my name.

I tried to open my eyes, wanting nothing more than to see Makoto one last time before it was all over.

Unfortunately, my body was no longer responding to the commands my brain was giving it.

I'm sorry. I love you.

My arm was abruptly yanked up, and something slender and hard was forced into my hand, my fingers numb beyond the point of being able to tell what it was. "If you won't do it, I will," Makoto rasped, his tone ... angry.

My kitsune forcefully kept the object in my palm, his fingers wrapped tightly around mine. I groaned, attempting to speak, but the words stuck in my throat. My arm jerked, once, twice, three times, followed by a gurgling sound. Something warm gushed over my hand, flowing down my exposed flesh. Chaotic beeps reverberated in my skull, dipping into one long final note. My brain revolted. *Miles. No!*

Releasing my hand, Makoto pushed me onto my back in one quick movement. His fingers slid over my forehead, forming symbols that burned into my skin. I convulsed, pain ripping through my veins ... no, my very soul.

I screamed, my world blotted out by blinding light.

R.

I JOLTED, sitting straight up, as if someone had electrocuted me awake. My gaze immediately snagged on Makoto, his lithe form standing so close to me that I could feel his body heat. I reached a hand up, recoiling when I saw the dried blood on it. My muscles tensed, fighting the urge to look in Miles' direction. It was a horror I didn't want to have etched into my retinas.

"Don't ... just don't, Rems. It was the only way."

I shook my head, my pulse pounding against my eardrums. "I was ready to die."

Makoto snorted. "Someone like you will never truly be ready to die."

My memories crystallized, as if the fog on my brain cleared suddenly. Pushing off the bed, I swayed into Makoto. I pawed at his chest, tears causing my surroundings to waver like watercolors. "Your heart. I don't understand. How are you alive?"

Makoto's arms tightened around me, his chin resting on the top of my head. "There's a reason why kitsunes are known as fox spirits. As you know I'm very much flesh and blood, at least here on this plane. Or maybe I should say, I can become spirit if I want to. It's hard to explain to someone who can't experience it. And I've never really had to talk about it before ... or needed to."

"So he didn't really steal your heart?" Hope danced within me, although I knew it was false. Kiernan wouldn't have ripped Makoto's beating heart from his chest for no reason.

"He stole the heart from my spirit self. I can technically live without it." He chuckled darkly. "As you can see for yourself."

"So what does it mean?"

"It's one of the ways zenko kitsune can become yako

kitsune. It means without my spirit heart I will become a dark kitsune ... yako ... unbalanced, wrong."

I pressed my face into his chest, swallowing around the lump in my throat. "How much time do we have?" Although a part of me wondered if he'd already begun changing. Would Makoto have taken Miles' life so easily, and without any signs of remorse otherwise? I may have always been morally ambiguous, but Makoto had never shared my mercenary attitude. Both sides of him served as a conscious to me when mine failed. *What'll happen if we both have broken moral compasses?*

"I'm not sure how long the transformation will take. Hopefully we won't have to find out."

I turned my head, the material of Makoto's kimono soft against my cheeks. "Blood magic," I murmured. "I knew what I had to do to live when I got out of Somniare, and yet somehow it didn't register ..."

"Kiernan tampered with your mind, but no matter what, it was the only way."

"We need to get out of here before anyone finds us with ... Miles. I'm no human hospital expert, but shouldn't nurses have come flying in or something when he flat-lined?" I pulled away from Makoto, carefully moving my gaze to the door. "I guess being in Somniare made me forget about ... reality. It's like time doesn't matter anymore."

"You'll readjust quickly." He grabbed my hand and yanked, my feet stumbling over themselves to follow him.

"Wait! I—" He turned to meet my gaze, his eyes indigo

instead of lavender, the sight jarring. I swallowed, running my free hand down my dress. "Just a second. Just one second."

I slid my eyes shut, quickly flipping through the things I knew in an attempt to center and focus myself. I'd been murdered by my own mother on the night of my ascension to be the next Grand Witch of Domus Novem. I'd escaped to the dreamscape of Somniare, thanks ultimately to Makoto. While there, I'd managed to rack up the fee of two favors, owed to a demon of unknown origin, who could come calling to collect at any moment. I'd discovered that I was tainted by dark magic, meaning I was a tenebris witch, and not grey at all like I'd believed. And Kiernan had stolen Makoto's spirit heart in order to ensure the quickest response possible on my part to find his magically imprisoned body in the real world. I shook my head, my heart quadrupling in speed. *Yep. No worries. I got this. All of it. Easy peasy.*

"Rems, we don't have time for this." Makoto's arm slid around my waist, tugging me into his side, his grip oppressive. "Come on. We need to get out of here."

My eyes fluttered open as Makoto spun me towards the door, my gaze passing over the hospital bed. "Oh, gods!" I sagged against his chest, clutching at his kimono, taking in exactly what I hadn't wanted to.

"Don't look." Makoto shifted to cover my eyes. "Just don't think about it."

But it was too late. Within the millisecond my gaze had darted over the scene, my brain had recorded everything. Miles' pallid complexion stood out in stark contrast to the red that he and his gown were seeped in, as if he'd been bathed in blood. His neck had lolled back on the pillow, the skin around the wound gaping—

I lurched to the side, bile erupting up my esophagus, burning my throat and mouth. A moment passed, maybe two, as the reality of what had become of Miles fully sank in. I dug my nails into Makoto's forearm, needing to ground myself. *Push it down. Push it all down. You didn't murder him. Not in the end. He offered his life for yours.* I couldn't let myself think about how I didn't deserve Miles' sacrifice; it would only cheapen what he'd done.

Allowing cold indifference to settle over me, I straightened my spine and slipped from Makoto's grasp. His fingers trailed over my arm, lingering in question, before falling away with uncertainty. "I'm fine now." I forced myself to lift my gaze to Miles again, or really, the empty shell that his soul had left behind.

I bowed in reverence. "Thank you, Miles. May you be blessed in the afterlife. I won't waste what you freely gave me." I whirled around, stalking from the room, but in my haste, instead of the exit, I found myself in a small bathroom.

I inhaled a sharp breath, my blue eyes ringed in white as they widened as far as they could go, their ridiculous state of surprise shown to me in the mirror hanging over the sink. At first, it was the runes etched in blood across my forehead that held my attention, drawing me to take a closer look, but those were expected on some level.

The thing that completely threw me for a loop … was me. My features. They were altered. I was me, and yet not.

"Makoto," I called. "Makoto—" I met his gaze in the reflection, even as my fingers skimmed my narrower nose, and higher cheekbones, pressing into the cleft in my chin before tracing over skinnier eyebrows.

"It happened after Miles gave his life-force to you. His intermingling with yours changed your outward appearance. I guess that's to be expected. All blood magic has a price. And that isn't much of one, if you ask me."

Dropping my hand, I averted my gaze. At first glance I hadn't even noticed, I was still me, and yet not. Which I was pretty sure was worse. It probably would have been easier to handle if I looked completely different, instead of just a bit … off. Not that any of it really mattered. *What if other things have*— I gulped, fear icing my spine. "Do you think anything else has changed?"

"Do you feel different?"

I turned my focus inward, sensing my magic was where it always had been, humming deep inside what felt like the core of me. "Not—no. Not that I can tell."

Makoto's warmth suffused my back as he wrapped his arms around me, his lips softly brushing my hair before his chin came to rest on the top of my head. I flicked my gaze back up to meet his in the reflection. "I don't care, in case you were wondering. I don't care if your appearance has been altered. You're alive, and that's all that matters to me. You're alive and you're still you on the inside. Which I could have told you, but I wanted you to check for yourself."

I leaned into him, a smile ghosting my lips. "Thanks. And it's not like I look hideous, or even that different. It's just ... jarring. I was startled. I—" My cheeks heated when I realized I'd merely wanted Makoto's approval. I could move past all of it because it didn't bother him. I wasn't sure if that made me shallow, or something much worse ... dependent.

"I get that." He spun me around, and steered me out the door, thankfully ignoring my inner turmoil, which I had no doubt he picked up on as my familiar. "But we really don't have time for this."

"Wait." I dragged my feet in an effort to stop us. "I should probably wash off the blood. It looks suspicious."

"It won't matter. It's all over you."

I glanced at my dress, nodding numbly. "Right. I forgot. I—" Biting my lip, I shook my head. "I guess I'm still a bit disoriented. Unless ... You don't think—"

"Your brain is fine, Rems. If anything in your head was affected by Miles, it'd probably be an improvement."

"Hey!" I slapped at his arm. "Take that back!"

Makoto tugged me into the hallway, a low chuckle rumbling through his chest. "I've never heard of anything internally being altered by such magic. I was kidding. Stop worrying."

"Not the time for jokes. If you—" I froze, Makoto following suit.

He dropped my arm and stepped forward, his

expression pinched with anxiety. "Now we know why no one came."

I blinked rapidly, processing our surroundings. There was a bubble of energy, bright blue and smooth, bowed outward around Miles' hospital room. Beyond the bubble … was carnage. Human nurses, doctors, and patients lay splayed in various depictions of death, blood and decay infecting all before us. "What the hell?" I muttered. It was as if they'd been fleeing something, something long gone, hopefully. My chest tightened. *I thought I left things like this back in Somniare.*

"It's definitely not a coincidence that someone supernatural put a protection spell around Miles' room. But who?" Without waiting for a response, I lifted my hands, pulling magic into them. I heaved a sigh of relief that I was able to use my powers again without worry of imminent death. Without thinking about it, I'd been restraining myself. It was another thing besides time that I was going to have to adjust back to since leaving Somniare.

My eyes fluttered shut as I concentrated. *Tell me who wove this spell.* I forced my energy outward, the protection bubble crackling with static electricity as I connected with it, all the fine hairs on my body rising. A flash of Kiernan's chiseled face skidded through my mind, his expression arrogant and mocking. My eyes snapped open, gaze immediately locking with Makoto's, who read the answer from my mind.

"Kiernan." He shook his head in disgust. "I

underestimated him from the beginning."

"We both did. But what's done is done."

A flash of purple revealed Makoto in fox form, his multilayered voice impatient when he commanded, "Break the spell and let's get back to Domus Novem ASAP."

I nodded, nibbling my thumbnail. He was right. Whatever had happened at the hospital was insignificant in comparison to what we were dealing with. We needed to get back to Domus Novem to gather resources for our upcoming ... journey? Quest? Missing goblin king search party? It wasn't that I didn't care about the dead humans, it was just ... well, I couldn't do anything for them now, so there was no point in wasting thoughts or emotions on the issue. My top priority was Makoto's missing spirit heart. The rest, even finding out why my own mother had murdered me, would have to wait until after I knew Makoto was safe.

I waved my hand, yanking at Kiernan's magic, breaking the spell. Pressure released as if a vacuum seal had been ripped open, my ears popping, and the stench of rot saturated the air.

Without another word, Makoto and I began to weave our way around blood-splattered and decomposing corpses, the pungent odor of death stifling.

I offered a silent blessing, hoping the humans all found the peace in their afterlives that had eluded them in life. Sometimes reality was far worse than nightmares. I would know.

Chapter 2

I sucked in lungful after lungful of fresh air, my throat dry and burning, while I balefully squinted at the sun. It was as if the sentient, faceless being was mocking me, lording cheer over the death-submerged land. My arms prickled with goose bumps despite the warmth penetrating my skin.

"A bit melodramatic, don't you think, Rems? Death-submerged land? Really? And sentient, faceless being mocking you? It's called the sun."

I scowled, waving my hand in the general direction of the hospital, where we'd beaten a hasty retreat from. "What would you call all of that then? Because it seemed pretty submerged in death to me. And we've talked about this before … if I don't say it out loud, I don't appreciate your commentary on my inner dialogue."

Indigo lupine eyes danced with mirth. "Sorry."

I snorted, shuffling across the pavement. "Yeah, you seem so sorry to me. I—"

"Shh ... did you hear that?" Makoto's ears swiveled, and its three tails lifted into the air as it spun its fox body in a circle, freezing to listen to something off to the right of us. "Fae. There are fae nearby. And they're heading in our direction."

"Fae? What kind?" I lifted my hands, building magic. I wouldn't be caught defenseless like in Somniare.

Makoto's ears pricked forward, eyes narrowing. "Not a good idea, Rems. There's three of them—light fae if I'm reading it right." My familiar's nostrils flared as it inhaled deeply. "Yes, royal guards of the Light Court. Too powerful for just the two of us." A flash of purple revealed Makoto in her original female form.

I resisted the urge to protest. I usually opted for a fight, but most days when I went against Makoto's advice, I regretted it. "What are you doing? If you don't think it's a good idea to fight, then shouldn't we be running?"

"I don't think we should necessarily run either ... "

I nodded. "Right. With them being so close to the hospital—the very human hospital—they have information." It wasn't the light fae style to murder so brutally. They hadn't been the ones to massacre the humans, that much I knew for sure.

"Exactly. And females always manage males best. We'll talk to them for a bit, find out what they know." She winked at me and I chortled. *Seriously, kitsunes are so sexist.*

But then again, if I was both sexes, maybe I would be, too. It's not like I could offend myself. Right?

I shook my head, dislodging my random musings. Of course, we were dealing with fae, who were about as old-fashioned as you could get, mostly because so many of them were as old as dirt. Being sexist, or expecting them to respond better to us as females since they were male, wasn't a ridiculous concept, sadly.

I rolled my shoulders, attempting to at least appear relaxed. "You mean flirt them into submission." I hated when Makoto flirted; it didn't matter with who, male or female. I had a jealous streak about a mile wide, which was difficult to contain. *But that was before we became ... more. Maybe I won't feel that way now that our intentions to be together have been declared.*

She shrugged, fighting a smile. I rolled my eyes, knowing she, and he for that matter, enjoyed my jealousy at times. As long as I didn't act on those irrational feelings. Makoto had never come out and said it, but she didn't have to. My kitsune liked evidence of how much I cared, even if up until recently, I had been led to believe that nothing would ever happen between us—besides want ... there had always been plenty of that.

"Have Tarik on a short lease, just in case," I muttered.

Forcing myself not to fidget, I pulled my magic as close as possible to the surface of my skin without it being visible, the heat of it reassuring. Dealing with Kiernan hadn't exactly strengthened my trust in fae. In fact, he'd managed to make me trust them less, something I hadn't thought possible.

Silence fell over us as the three fae in question strode into sight from around the edge of the building. My nerves hummed with trepidation, my heart stuttering in my chest before setting off at a gallop. They were definitely royal guards of the Light Court. Their white gold armor adorned with Celtic script and the accompanying starburst on the chest plate, which was the symbol of the Light Court, confirmed it. Regardless, I would have known what they were just by how they held themselves—heads high, posture rigid, jewel-toned eyes cold and arrogant, glittering with disdain. Each purposeful stride contained the kind of swagger that only Light Court royal guard seemed to possess, as if they were too good for ... everyone, and yet they wanted you to look anyways, to desire to touch. To covet them at all times.

Fae magic beat against my senses as they closed the gap between us. The scent of it surged up my nose, too sweet and oppressive, as the taste of honey drowned my taste buds, my skin tingling as if a thousand tiny fingers caressed me all at once. I smirked, resisting the lure of it, knowing it was all part of the show. 'Look how beautiful and powerful we are. Bow before us. Desire us. Give us whatever we want.' *Not gonna happen. Ever.*

"Oh, look, Makoto, light fae. Do you think they wanted to visit the hospital to have the sticks removed from their ass—"

Makoto's elbow connected with my ribs. "Stop it. Flirt, not insult. Do I need to get you a dictionary?"

She shot me a glare before stepping forward, a grin plastered on her face as she flipped her white hair over her shoulder. "Hello there." She wiggled the tips of her fingers in a tiny wave. "We were hoping you could help us." She tilted her head and bit her lip, causing me to stifle a groan of irritation. There was no way they were going to fall for—

One of the guards streaked towards us, a blur of color. He stopped mere inches in front of Makoto, delivering her a dazzling smile meant to charm. "A kitsune. It's been some time since I've seen one of your kind. What brings you and this," he narrowed his sapphire eyes in my direction, "*cailleach*, here?" The faint lilt to his voice somehow managed to be beautiful, despite the words. It was distinctly fae; almost Irish, yet not, a bit Scottish, but not as rough. The cadence was musical and yet primal at the same time. I'd decided long ago that the fae accent was part of their seduction. It was the only way for such ugly, vile words to be received so enthusiastically by so many. It almost didn't matter what was murmured in one's ear, the song was still beautiful, just like all deadly things. "And how may I be of service to *you*?" He bowed low, his platinum hair gleaming in the sun like spun silk.

"How may *we* be of service to you?" The other two guards appeared at their companion's side, flanking him. Each of them was stunningly beautiful, like all fae. Their eyes the color of jewels—sapphire, emerald, and topaz swirled with interest at Makoto, setting my teeth on edge.

The fae on the left ran his elegant, slender hand down Makoto's arm, lingering a bit too long for my taste. I chewed on the inside of my cheek to keep from commenting on the whole *cailleach* thing. Of course, I hadn't really expected them to be excited to see me, a lowly witch.

I tried to smile, but my lips curled back from my teeth in a sneer. Still, I persisted in my subpar attempt at flirting. "We were hoping you could help us. You see—"

"No one asked you to speak, *cailleach*."

"That's not very nice," Makoto admonished. "After all, I belong to her."

"Not possible," the handsy fae murmured, his fingers curling around Makoto's cheek. "Kitsunes belong to no one."

She giggled. "I do belong to her. But she belongs to me, too." Makoto sidestepped, reaching for me, taking my hand in hers.

Three sets of jeweled gazes moved from Makoto to me, and then back again, the leches processing what she was implying. Emerald eyes locked with mine, and I shivered from the intensity. "Well then … what can we do for the both of you?" Magic danced over my skin, pooling in my center, warming me in ways I preferred not to acknowledge.

I forced down the revulsion from what emerald-eyes was suggesting. *Friggin' fae pervs.* I'd heard stories about their orgies. "What are you doing here, openly moving about the human realm without any glamour?"

"Hopefully about to have some fun," sapphire-eyes said, leaning closer to Makoto. Her hand tightened around mine, threatening to cut off the circulation. "You do like fun, don't you?"

"But first, someone needs to … clean up." Topaz-eyes snapped his fingers, and I knew without checking that I had been given the equivalent of a magical bath—every part of me, including my clothes, would now be spotless. Such magic was frivolous, or at least that's what I'd been raised to believe. The fae … well, their entire existence was one frivolity after another. *Although I'd be lying if I said it wasn't a relief to have Miles' blood gone from my skin.*

Emerald eyes captured me in their swirling green depths, making it impossible to look away. I swallowed, my skin suddenly overheated, my clothes too constrictive. I yanked my hand from Makoto's, tearing at my dress, wanting—no, needing to strip.

Stop. Concentrate. You're letting him roll your mind to his will. You're stronger than that. But the urge to drink of the fae's lips, to run my tongue over his skin—to let him touch me wherever and however he wanted, it was the only way to satisfy what my body craved. It was the only way to stop my imminent combustion. *His will is my own.*

Inky darkness overtook everything, plunging the world into the unknown. A sudden flash of light illuminated the fae guards, causing the air to stick in my lungs as I struggled to breathe. They were covered in blood—dark crimson dripping off noses, ears, and fingertips—eyes milky and lifeless. And yet there they stood on their own power, dead, and yet not, their lips moving silently to form words I couldn't decipher.

I whipped my head in Makoto's direction, another flash of light revealing her face. Her eyes glinted red with anger, a malicious sneer twisting her features, as her hair —her *black* hair lifted to swirl around her, crackling with magic.

"No!" I stumbled back. Magic, dark magic, pulsated around me, plummeting me into unconsciousness.

I GROANED, my mouth as dry as the Sahara, and my brain sluggish, as if it was filled with cotton candy. I fought to remember where I was and what had happened to knock me out.

My body vibrated with tension when it all rushed back to me, the image of Makoto surrounded by death and dark magic. I squeezed my eyes shut tighter, not wanting to wake up if that was the reality I would one day be forced to face.

Fear, slow and steady, slithered up my spine, causing my adrenaline to surge. *No. Stop. Fear is a four-letter word. Makoto is your familiar—your friend—your partner—the other half of your soul.* What I'd seen was linked to Makoto's stolen spirit heart. It was a vision of what *could* come, not of what was destined to be. Which meant my kitsune could be fixed—*would* be fixed. I would save us. I would make everything right ... somehow.

Forcing my breathing to regulate, I opened my eyes. Sun streamed down, filtered through a canopy of trees overhead, causing me to squint. "Makoto," I rasped.

"I'm right here, Rems." Her angular face came into view above mine, indigo eyes edged with gold, the only physical evidence of her worry.

I reached up to entwine my fingers in her comfortingly white hair, tugging her down to me. *It's not too late ... yet.* Without thought, or really, without care, I pressed my lips to hers fiercely, needing to forget, if only for a moment, the image of my kitsune so altered by dark magic. *Her* dark magic if I didn't save her.

Her fingers trailed up my ribcage, skirting my flesh where it was most sensitive. She gasped into my mouth when I flipped us, wrapping her legs around my waist, and covering her body with mine. "I won't lose you again," I whispered against her skin, the taste of it sweet, and oh-so addictive.

Because that's exactly what had happened in Somniare, even though I hadn't known it at first. When my memories had been swiped of Makoto, I hadn't remembered anything about her. She'd hidden behind other forms ... her fox, humans she'd seen, all in an attempt to keep from triggering what was still in my heart. Now that I had her back, nothing short of death could rip her from me.

"Never again. You'll never lose me again. I swear it."

AVA WIXX

I slid my hands underneath her kimono, kneading her thighs as I rocked against her. "I love you. All of you." Desperation rode me hard. I was afraid ... so afraid of losing the one person who meant everything to me. Promises meant nothing. I knew that. Only time would tell what truly lay ahead for us.

Makoto arched her neck back, breaking our kiss so she could speak. "Rems, we can't do this now. Not here. And not with an audience."

Audience? I froze. *Shit. The royal fae guards.* Their energy hummed around us, leaving me to wonder how much of my actions had really been my choice, and how much had been driven by their magic. Not that I wouldn't have happily continued what I started with Makoto, but I wasn't one for spontaneous displays of lust out in the open. Especially not when so much was on the line.

I'd trained to be able to thwart seduction by way of fae magic. Normally, it was child's play, but apparently, I was still a bit off since thwarting death itself. It was another reason why fae were so dangerous. Their magic enticed and beguiled, gently persuading its victim to bend to their will. It was easier to be led astray by the promise of pleasure than to be forced into submission, especially when it's gradual. I hadn't noticed it taking hold of me, and I still wasn't sure where my desires began and the faes' ended. *Maybe there isn't much of a difference at the moment.* That thought was sobering.

I stood, crossing my arms over my chest as I met the jeweled gazes of each fae in turn. "Sorry, boys, playtime is over. You're just going to have to find your kicks elsewhere."

Sapphire-eyes snorted. "Playtime has just begun, *cailleach.*"

"Is this what you do when unsupervised?"

The fae guards scurried from their seats on a fallen tree to their feet, comically fast. Sapphire-eyes raised his chin, replying, "No, my liege."

With a flash of purple, my kitsune was back to fox form, pressing its warm fur into my side. I rested my hand on its head, intrigued by the scene unfolding before us.

"Then explain yourselves."

Sapphire-eyes stepped forward and bowed, but my gaze traveled to the figure emerging from the forest, instant recognition jolting my system. *The crown prince of the Light Court.* I'd never seen him outside of Alternum before, which was what we witches referred to the realm the fae called home. It literally translated to 'other world'. *Personally, I'd always thought Land of the Asshats would have been more fitting.* But it had been named so long ago, that attempting to call it anything else never stuck, so Alternum was the fae realm and Mundi was ours.

The prince was tall, at least six foot four, but seemingly larger by way of presence. His platinum hair was intricately braided and pulled away from his strong, chiseled features, highlighting his rugged jawline, and pointed ears. Diamond eyes glittered, catching the light, as they flitted around, taking in everything. His skin was golden and flawless, his lithe muscles encased in white leather enriched with silver detailing, something I was pretty sure only one such as him could pull off. The crown prince of the Light Court was what one would call savagely beautiful, and yet he was refined by fae elegance, a study in contrasts, just like all of his race.

"My liege, we—we grew bored. The creature we seek hasn't returned, and with no magical traces to track it … our apologies."

Ignoring the guards, the crown prince, known otherwise as Prince Anyon, focused in on me, bowing his head slightly, barely more than a mere nod. "My apologies to you both."

One of the guards sucked in a sharp breath, affronted by the display of submission by their prince, to me, a *cailleach*. Suspicion swamped me. "Mmm hmm … so what do you want from us," I curtsied demonstratively, "Prince Anyon?"

The prince's full lips curled up, his eyes sparkling with suppressed laughter. "Ah, you have not changed, my dear Remy." His gaze raked me from head to toe. "At least not on the inside."

It'd been years since I'd laid eyes on Prince Anyon. I'd been awestruck by him as a young teen, falling all over myself to capture his attention. He was the fae who had truly taught me how cruel his kind could be. His flawless beauty was introduced to me as part of my training, a favor owed to my family, one collected with a price, and yet I would be forever in his debt to have been given it.

He'd made me stronger, but not before breaking me down.

Makoto's tails tickled my ankles, reminding me that my familiar had been there for me then, and was here for me now. "Oh, but I have changed on the inside, too. I'm not a naïve little witchling anymore."

The prince quirked one perfectly arched eyebrow and clucked his tongue. "And yet you seemed to be under the thrall of my guards when I arrived. How ... embarrassing. For you."

Yep. There's the Prince Anyon I know, and despise. "I'd already broken free, which I'm sure you're conveniently pretending to have missed." I ran my hands through my hair. "I've had a long couple of ..." I frowned, not knowing how long I'd been in Somniare. "Well, I'm not sure how long I was gone, but I'm still adjusting to this realm. It took me a moment to get my magical bearings. But, I assure you, I'll be back to normal soon."

Prince Anyon crouched, ignoring my denial of being controlled by the fae guards, his face level with Makoto's fox snout. "And I see your faithful companion is still by your side." He tilted his head, eyeing my kitsune. "But hiding from me? Why?"

"I'm not hiding," Makoto snapped, sharp canines flashing. "You know as well as anyone that the fox is my true animal form."

"Yes, but I also know how much you enjoy being one of your true human forms when you're with her." He nodded once in my direction. "Or have you forgotten how much I learned about the two of you when I was ... introduced to her."

I'd long suspected Prince Anyon had ulterior motives when it came to my training. Regardless of what was owed, it was nearly impossible to get a fae to do something that they were opposed to. I was pretty sure he'd wanted intel on the next Grand Witch of Domus Novem, in case I ever became a problem. He hadn't had to dig very far, though—my greatest weakness, and strength, always had and always would be my love for Makoto. Of course, that love had matured a bit since the last time we'd seen him. Friendship had grown into a blooming relationship.

Prince Anyon was right. Makoto was hiding from him. Even though he'd witnessed the tail end of our little groping session, the prince probably thought it was more fae magical coercion than us. It was definitely better to keep him in the dark about the truth, if it was possible. A relationship, at least the kind that had developed between Makoto and myself, was considered taboo, wrong. That perception was not limited to the domos magicae. The fae would be just as swift to condemn our relationship, punishing us however they saw fit. Obviously, the royal guards hadn't realized that Makoto was technically my familiar since kitsunes normally didn't bond themselves in any subservient way to any creature. *Clearly, they're not very smart.* Prince Anyon, on the other hand, was very intelligent, and we would have to be careful around him.

"No one has forgotten anything." *We'll always be*

enemies, no matter the pretenses that surround us. I turned my mind away from the unwanted image of me grinning up at Prince Tall, Glittering, and Conceited when we'd first met, hoping furiously that he'd be my first kiss. *Now that's embarrassing.* "Although I wish I could," I mumbled under my breath.

Prince Anyon pulled himself up to his full height, his head thrown back in laughter, the melody rich and deep. I couldn't help but watch, marveling at how stunning he was. "Still an open book." I shrunk away from him as he crowded my personal space, causing me to lean into Makoto who held steady. The prince's fingers pinched my chin as he lifted my gaze to meet his. "But you were so delightful back when I got to know you—all smiles, and blushing cheeks. Maybe if you would have been a bit more mature, like now, I would have—"

Magic buzzed in my right hand, just before Tarik popped into existence, the angry red glow casting Prince Anyon in a menacing light, the blade pressed to his throat before I made the conscious thought to move. "Back off, your highness," I growled. "If you have a purpose for being here, let it be known. I'm not about to trade your guards' games for yours."

Diamond eyes crystallized, and darkened. "Nice to see you again as well, Tarik." The prince placed his hand over mine on the hilt of the sword, my fingers spasming. Somehow I managed to hold on, if not barely; something I'd never been able to do before against the onslaught of the prince's magic.

I smirked. "As I was saying, your royal prince-ness, tell me what you want before my patience wears thin."

He reached up and tucked an errant strand of hair behind my ear. "No armor? Slacking, Tarik? Or are you just that arrogant now?" He lifted his hands into the air and backed up a few steps. "Sheath your claws, little *cailleach*, and we can talk. No more games. For now."

I knew that was the best I would get from a fae, the promise of no games for the time being. I nodded, before releasing Tarik, mentally thanking him for having my back, as always.

"All right, so let's talk."

Chapter 3

Prince Anyon waved his arm, sending the guards away with nothing more than a faint audible pop. "It's so hard to find good help," he grumbled, before settling in to lean against a large oak tree. *Why do fae always seem to do that? Lean, lounge ... it's like their natural state is reclining in some manner. Lazy, arrogant asshats.*

I glanced around warily, my chest tightening with an unshakable feeling of foreboding. *Something's not right.* The forest itself exuded an ominous energy, as if the natural order of things had been tampered with. I nibbled on my thumbnail, causing Makoto to knock against me subtly, but with intent. "Sorry," I muttered, dropping my hand. Makoto had been trying to get me to stop biting my nails for years. My kitsune claimed it was a nasty habit that showcased my nerves to enemies. It wasn't a completely unfounded line of thought. It kind of went hand in hand with the adage 'never let them see you sweat'.

"Why are you and Makoto here?"

"Us? Why are you and your fae brethren skulking around the human realm without glamour? Did I miss the proclamation that fae could do that legally now? Last I checked it was in everyone's best interest to keep our world secret from the humans. And what about that horror movie scene in the hospital ... what the hell happened?"

Prince Anyon shifted, crossing his legs at the ankles. "Humans know of witches and fae. Some always have."

I rolled my eyes. "You know that's not what I mean. Some humans suspect. Even others buy our spells, but ... proof? None of them have concrete proof. Even when a spell works for a human, which if Domus Novem made it then it most certainly would, we never sell anything flashy —anything that couldn't be written off as a kook believing in things that don't exist. But you know this, you know all of this. So what's this about? Just tell me what you know about the hospital."

Prince Anyon studied me a moment, searching for I wasn't sure what, his face a mask of indifference. "How long were you away? And where were you?" He leaned forward ever so slightly, belying more interest in my answer than he'd probably meant to.

"Somniare. I was in Somniare. And I already told you, I don't know how long I was there. Things were ... complicated. Still are in fact."

My skin prickled with awareness, goose bumps rising in quick succession. I flicked my gaze to the dense woods behind us, unable to shake the feeling of being watched. Maybe that's what I'd been feeling before? Someone or something was in the forest that shouldn't be, the energy of it all wrong.

Something's spying on us, I thought at Makoto, not wanting whatever it was to know that I was on to it.

Makoto's tails uncurled, raising high in the air, eyes and ears focused on the patch of forest where our visitor was lurking. Prince Anyon relaxed his body, but his forehead creased with tension. He gave me a slight nod, letting me know that he was aware of the situation as well.

"How complicated?" he asked, keeping up the pretenses of our conversation.

Makoto flew into the woods, a blur of color, purple mist in its wake as the fox became its original male form, wielding an indigo-glowing Tarik. Snarls erupted from the thicket, quickly silenced by one slice of his sentient katana's blade.

Both Prince Anyon and I dashed towards Makoto, magic at the ready. "It's fine," Makoto called. "It was a *Cu Sith*." He stood, his kimono fluttering in the breeze as he yanked the dark form out into the open.

I stared in disbelief. *A Cu Sith—a demon dog of fae origin.* Its presence explained the weird juju I'd been experiencing, since it was not of our world, and definitely didn't belong in the forest. I'd never seen a *Cu Sith* in person, only drawn within the pages of books. Its compact body was no bigger than a medium-sized domestic dog, thirty or forty pounds at most. Its claws and teeth were long and sharp, glinting in the subdued light like onyx knives. "What the hell? How did it get here?"

Prince Anyon bent over to study the dead creature, petting its midnight fur with reverence. "The *Cu Sith* should be respected. Like so many things of my realm, it's misunderstood, and not any more dangerous than say a wolf, or a mountain lion."

Makoto bowed his head. "I would never kill such a majestic creature without good reason." He opened his palm to reveal a golden collar. "But this one was sent here, and I wasn't going to wait around for it to attack."

Prince Anyon stared at the collar, silent. I poked him with my index finger, wanting answers. "Is this what you had your guards looking for? Is this *Cu Sith* the thing that killed all the humans at the hospital? Who was controlling it?" The golden collar meant the *Cu Sith* had been bespelled to do another's will. It may have been sent merely to be ears and eyes for its master, but Makoto was right to kill it under the circumstances.

He heaved a sigh. "No. This was yet another surprise. And honestly, I'm getting tired of them."

"You need to explain … everything."

He sighed again, not meeting my gaze. "You're not wrong. It seems as though many things are not what they seem." He snatched the golden collar from Makoto, clenching it tightly as sudden anger rolled off of him in palpable waves. "Come, we'll have that talk now, but not here. Not out in the open."

"Then where?" My stomach somersaulted, already suspecting the answer.

"As if you have to ask, my dear little Remy."

R.

I GRITTED MY TEETH, fighting to remain calm. "You know I hate this place. I don't … I don't think I can handle this right now." I nibbled at my nails before forcing my hands to my sides, balling them into fists. "Seriously, Makoto, I'm about to lose my damn mind."

We were in a box. Well, not actually. It was a square space made up of fae magic, Prince Anyon's to be specific, that when used, was impenetrable by any other magical being. No one would know we were in it, and no one could hear what we spoke of inside. The prince had used such a place when training me. He might have owed my family a favor, but he wanted no witnesses to him working with a lowly witch. He obviously wanted privacy now but had left Makoto and me alone for what felt like hours.

Makoto didn't move from his sitting position on the floor. "He always did like to push your buttons. Not that it's difficult."

I glared at my kitsune, who was much too calm for my taste. "Fine. While we're waiting for the royal pain in my ass, how about we discuss what happened back there?"

Makoto lifted his head, gaze locking with mine. "Care to specify?"

Is he thinking about our kisses, or the way—

I swallowed, suddenly overheated. *Nope. Not the time for that.* "Yeah, when we were talking to the three royal guards, and I had that vision. And don't try to deny how I got it. We both know it was triggered by your thoughts—your very murderous thoughts. Did you want me to see it, or was it just that strong?"

He stared at the ground. "I don't—I really don't know if I wanted you to see it. I was overwhelmed, drowning in dark emotions ... urges. Well, I had those ... urges because of my missing spirit heart."

"Mmm hmm ... I already guessed the part about your missing heart being the root of the problem. But what made you so ... so angry?"

Before I could even blink, I found myself caged in by Makoto's larger form, his nose touching mine, and our heated breath intermingling. His spicy, rich scent—the quality of it indefinable and yet instantly recognizable to me as home—coiled around me, both calming and inciting in equal parts. "You're mine, Rems. I wanted to rip them limb from limb for what they wanted to do to you." His eyes darkened before they fired gold, his fingers curling into the wall like claws. "He was rolling your mind, and I couldn't handle it."

He shoved himself off the wall, turning away, his shoulders hunched. Knowing it wasn't the time or place, I stopped myself from pulling him back to me, craving the physical attention he so clearly wanted to give me. "I would have resisted. I just needed a moment to gather my strength. What I said to Prince Anyon wasn't a lie, I'm still a bit off since Somniare." I sucked in a shaky breath, my forehead burning from phantom letters made up of Miles' blood. "I almost died all the way." I swiped my hand across my face, half expecting it to come away with blood. It didn't, of course. I was clean … at least physically.

"It's the imbalance. I'm imbalanced now. I can't explain how—I just can't, Rems. We need to fix me. We need to fix me before it gets worse and I do something I regret."

Prince Anyon appeared in the middle of the room, his gaze shifting between the two of us. "Both of you are … not right. Did you think I wouldn't notice?" He fluttered his hand at me. "You look different from more than just aging, your features have changed. And you," he stepped closer to Makoto, tilting his head, "are darker. Your energy is darker. You're becoming—"

"A yako kitsune, I know," Makoto growled, his eyes flashing black.

"I told you it was complicated. Now, tell me what was so important that you brought us here." My lips curled back from my teeth involuntarily.

Prince Anyon inclined his head. "Very well, I'll get right to the point. It has finally begun."

"What's finally begun?" *Vague much?*

"The war that all magical beings have been fearing since the beginning of time. The war between light and dark. The war that could end everything as we know it."

Sweat gathered on my upper lip and around my hairline, even though it felt as if the temperature had dropped about ten degrees. "What?"

Makoto glanced at me before addressing the prince, his complexion waxen. "How do you know? There have been times before—"

"Not like this!" Prince Anyon thundered. "Entire domos magicae have been wiped out. Humans are being slaughtered out in the open. Tears are appearing in the fabric between realms. Important fae assassinated. And those are just the highlights. No, I'm sure it has begun this time."

"When? How?" I wanted to ask another question. One much more important, but I couldn't. I just couldn't.

"Domus Novem is lost to you." But apparently I didn't need to ask. "You are the last witch from any grey coven to be alive. They were taken out by the tenebris houses. It was the beginning. No one was prepared."

I sucked in air through my nostrils, my teeth so tightly clenched my jaw began to ache, my emotions and words lost inside of me. *I feel nothing. Absolutely nothing.*

A memory from Somniare slammed into me.

One by one the bodies shuddered and moved, ambling to their feet. I was paralyzed with panic as they started shuffling towards me, arms outstretched. They weren't zombies, not really, but they were close enough. "No! I didn't do anything!"

"Exactly. You didn't do anything!"

I pressed my palms into my eyes, rubbing. None of that was real. It was all part of the nightmare I'd been living in Somniare. Unless … unless the things I'd seen there, my mother stabbing me, the dead Novem witches … What if I'd known all of it was true on some level? What if the nightmares in Somniare had merely been my magic picking up on the truth, and trying to communicate it to me in the only way it could at the time? After all, my mother had turned out to be the one who murdered me, and now …

A wave of nausea crashed into me, washing away the numbness that had been encasing me. "No. No, no, no, no, no. I didn't do anything. They were right. I didn't save them." I dropped to my knees, unable to erase from my mind's eye the images of my dead friends and family as zombie-like creatures.

Prince Anyon wrenched my arms away from my face, his eyes fierce. "How did you escape? Tell me how the two of you got out when no one else did. What happened to the two of you, and why did you show up outside that hospital? Now? Whatever killed those people slipped through a rift between realms nearby. Do you know what it was, or where it went? Did you bring it with you?"

Could I have brought something out of Somniare with us? Had Kiernan left the protection spell outside Miles' room because he knew something like that could or would happen? Was it all connected to blood magic? *I'm in so over my head.* Laughter bubbled up and erupted from me. "How did we escape? Don't you know? I'm a tenebris witch. Always have been. So I guess there are no grey witches left after all." Blue flames sprung from my hands,

racing up my arms. "I'm not what you thought I was."
Thanks to Kiernan.

"Rems, no!" Makoto knocked me away from the prince
before I could inadvertently injure him, my flames not
dangerous to Makoto since he was my familiar.

My eyes burned as I stared up into Makoto's face. His
countenance softened as he gently stroked the curve of
my cheek with his fingertips. "It'll be okay. All of it. I
promise." He pressed his supple lips to my forehead, and
peace settled over me as my eyes fluttered shut.

Chapter 4

I didn't remember opening my eyes, but my vision was filled, my attention riveted to the beating heart lying in the palm of Kiernan's leather-clad hand. Everything else around me was a blur.

Thump-thump, thump-thump, thump-thump ...

"What do you want?" I demanded, not lifting my gaze from Makoto's spirit heart.

"You know what I want."

I dug my nails into my palms, vibrating with the effort it took to remain still, knowing it wouldn't do any good to try and snatch the heart from Kiernan. *I won't give you the satisfaction of failing.* "Then why are you waylaying any progress I could be making by bringing me here?" I'd realized almost instantly that I'd lost consciousness, and Kiernan had seized the opportunity to pull me into Somniare.

"I wanted to remind you what's at stake."

Fury shot through me, boiling my blood. "I know what's at stake! You don't have to remind me!"

"Do not reveal my existence to Prince Anyon."

Ah, so that's what this is about. "Fine," I spat. "Is that all?" I hadn't planned on telling the prince, regardless of what Kiernan thought. I didn't trust Prince Anyon any more than I did Kiernan.

"I'm going to send a gift to you. Don't question it. Use it." Kiernan's other hand cupped overtop Makoto's heart, concealing it from view even though its steady rhythm still filled my ears.

Thump-thump, thump-thump, thump-thump ...

"Remember, like magic calls to like magic. Use mine to find my body."

That was the reason Kiernan had begun feeding me his magic all those years ago. He'd planned to use me from the first moment Makoto had come to him to bargain for my life. Without Kiernan's magic intermingling with mine in my blood, without it truly being a part of me, I would have had no way to find him in the real world. *So why did he never try using anyone else? Did he never have the opportunity? Or maybe he had found someone, maybe many someones, and they'd all failed.*

Thump-thump, thump-thump, thump-thump ...

The strong, steady cadence of Makoto's spirit heart filled me, blotting out everything else.

Thump-thump, thump-thump, thump-thump...

I sat up, my forehead hitting Makoto's chin. "Ow," he grumbled. "You need to stop doing that."

I scowled, rubbing the point of impact. "I'd be happy to stop hitting into you after losing consciousness. More than happy, in fact, to stop losing consciousness against my will, and lying in a heap like a sack of trash wherever I fall. Maybe that's your cue to stop using your stupid kitsune ways to knock me out cold. You're not doing either of us any favors."

Makoto matched my scowl, glaring. "You needed a chance to rest your mind, to refocus. You were about to have a magical meltdown." He tugged at one of the braids in his hair. "And I was protecting you—watching you very carefully. I would never just let you lie there."

Did Makoto know that while my body had remained in reality, my spirit had been in Somniare with Kiernan? He didn't give any signs that he did. I decided to ask him later when we had some privacy. I sighed, rubbing my temples. "All right, fine."

And although not part of Makoto's plan, seeing Kiernan had refocused me on my ultimate goal. I'd mourn my friends and family later, there was no time for it now. I couldn't save them, any of them … but I still had a chance to fix Makoto. *No point crying over what can't be changed.*

"Are we done with the dramatics?" Prince Anyon asked, his tone bored. He, of course, was lounging against the wall.

"Dramatics?" I squeaked. "I just found out my entire domos magicae was slaughtered, and I don't even—"

"Enough." The prince's cool gaze clashed with mine. "You're not the only one who has ever lost loved ones. But we have other matters to speak of that are much more pressing."

I sneered, sliding out from Makoto's grasp. "What does a fae know of love?"

The walls themselves shifted, crackling with energy, Prince Anyon's features clouding over. "Just because we love differently, does not mean we do not love."

Makoto moved to stand between us, his arms outstretched. "This will get us nowhere, fast. Both of you let it go. Now."

"Your ... *familiar* is right. We have much more important things to discuss."

I stilled, my eyes widening. The way he'd hesitated on calling Makoto my familiar—

He knows.

A slow smile curled the prince's lips up, an acknowledgement and challenge intermingled. "I'm not a fool like my guards. All one has to do is pay attention to how the two of you interact for a moment, and the truth is there for all to see."

"You can't tell anyone, ple—" I wouldn't lower myself to begging. Either he intended to flap his stupid fae gums about it, or he didn't. He was probably already planning on using the knowledge against us somehow, as leverage for something he wanted. It was the way of the fae.

Prince Anyon's lower lip stuck out in a faux pout. "Aw. Not to worry, my dear Remy, I'll keep your secret ... if you keep mine."

I pinched the bridge of my nose, exhaling long and loud. "Of course, and what secret would that be?"

He glided forward, his feet barely touching the ground, pausing in front of Makoto. The prince, while maintaining eye contact with me, gently cupped my kitsune's cheek. "I can see the appeal. Your *familiar* really is stunning in both of his human forms." He leaned into Makoto, brushing his lips along his jaw. I stiffened, grinding my teeth together. "Let me know if you ever grow tired of her, you're always welcome in my bed, male or female in form."

"Kitsunes mate for life," Makoto rasped, staring up into the prince's sparkling eyes.

"Mate? With a *cailleach*? But she will grow old and die."

"It doesn't matter. She's the only one I'll ever want."

Prince Anyon moved past Makoto, his gaze fully focused on me again. "Or is that even true anymore? Now that you dabble in black magic? Maybe you won't age and you'll remain as young and lovely as you are now, forever."

"I don't *dabble* in black magic!" But even as the words left my mouth, the lie tasted bitter on my tongue. My thoughts flashed to the demon to who I owed two favors to already. Was it worse to dabble when I didn't know what I was doing rather than throw myself in wholeheartedly? I could live practically forever with Makoto, and not age a day if I merely learned how to do the magic. *Should I? Should I learn? Maybe it's doing more harm to remain ignorant than not at this point.*

"Despite what you say, you are not a true tenebris witch, at least not yet."

"Enough of all this crap. Why is it always like this with fae? Huh? Just tell me your damn secret already so I can keep it or whatever."

The prince ignored my outburst and crowded me like he'd just done to Makoto. "I've always liked you, Remy. You would be welcome in my bed as well."

I slapped his hand before it could make contact with my skin. *Stupid fae thinking that any touch from him is invited. Ha!* "Makoto and I would be welcome in your bed? How about that. Good to know. Because you'd never be welcome in ours!" Prince Anyon blinked at me as if he couldn't process my words. "Yeah, that's right, your royal assholey-ness. Hard for you to understand, I get that, but we *don't* want you. Get over yourself."

"Rems," Makoto chastised, his eyes darting around our potential prison.

"My mother, the queen, is dead."

My mouth fell open. It hung there for a few moments before I found my voice. "The Queen of the Light Court is dead?"

"Yes, but no one knows. I've been trying to keep it a secret to avoid the panic that it will surely cause among my people." He turned to pace the small space. "I never wanted to be king. And as far as anyone knows, nothing has changed. I'm still just the crown prince. I was happy letting my mother make the hard decisions while I got—"

"While you did whatever you wanted. Yes, I seem to

remember exactly how spoiled you are, or were," Makoto said. "So if no one knows, why tell us? We're not exactly your ... friends."

"But you're not my enemies either." He eyed me thoughtfully before continuing, "And with the way things are, that's as good as it may get for me for the foreseeable future. I don't know who to trust anymore. Someone murdered my mother and I don't have a clue how or what they would stand to gain from it."

I pushed my annoyance at Prince Anyon aside for the time being. "And what do you expect us to do about it? My entire family has been murdered. I'm not exactly rolling deep in allies myself at the moment."

Prince Anyon dropped his head. "I need your help."

I wanted to laugh. First Kiernan, and now the crown prince—or I guess the soon-to-be King of the Light Court. Two of the most powerful fae in existence, and they both wanted my help. I wasn't sure if that was irony, but it sure felt like it. "Again, what can *I* do?"

Black smoke poured into the room, submerging us into darkness. I instinctively covered my nose and mouth with my sleeve, reaching for protective magic. Before I had the chance to cast any spell, I felt Makoto slide his arm around my waist.

"Unlock this room," Makoto coughed out. "Now."

"I can't," Prince Anyon rasped. "Something's blocking my magic."

So much for this place being untraceable and impenetrable. I guess nothing is truly infallible, not even fae magic. And if

Prince Anyon's magic was blocked then surely mine was as well. I reached for it just in case, or rather being driven by irrational hope. However, just as I'd expected, nothing came when I called.

"Tarik! We need you!" He didn't come either. I internally cursed myself for not considering that if we couldn't get out, Tarik couldn't get in. *Shit. Now what?*

Panic swept through me. The air in the room heated, the dark now illuminated by golden and red flames. *I will not burn to death in this friggin' box.*

"Try harder!" I screeched at Prince Anyon.

"I can't," Prince Anyon croaked, the sound of defeat in his voice.

I stepped forward, snatching through the smoke for the prince, my hands finally finding the front of his shirt. I shook hard. "What the hell is wrong with you? Since when do you give up? Get us out of here!"

As I rifled through my mind grasping at anything that could possibly save us, the knowledge of what I needed to do sprung to life in that calm, quiet place—the place that knew things like how to use blood magic.

I grabbed Prince Anyon by his hair, wrenching him towards me before he could react. I pressed my lips to his, biting savagely.

"Rems! What—"

"Just stay out of my way, Makoto!"

I ran my fingers along the weeping gouge in the prince's lip, stealing what I needed to form the symbols on my forearm, since there was no better place to draw them at the moment, the floor already too hot. *Please let this work.*

Time stopped, and two eyes resembling the ends of lit cigarettes appeared before me, its body blending with the smoke in the room.

Laughter rumbled through my mind, dark and inky.

I nodded once. "Just get us out of here."

"That's three favors."

"I know," I muttered. "I know."

Chapter 5

W hen time restarted, the three of us—Prince Anyon, Makoto, and myself—stood in front of a wrought iron gate. In the center was the symbol for Domus Novem, similar to a Celtic knot in appearance, the curves twisted into nine points, the pattern itself lopsided and stretching to blend with the dark metal of the gate itself. It proudly declared who owned the property without being ostentatious about it. The gate stood as a silent sentry, the first defense against any unwanted guests. It was my home. Or it had been. Once the house beyond the gate would have been all lit up, bustling at any hour, day or night. Now it was dark, death's touch having left its fingerprints on everything.

"How did we get here?" Prince Anyon demanded.

I lifted my gaze to Makoto's, black ringing the indigo in them. He was afraid for me. He knew what I'd done, and he wasn't even aware of the new favor I owed, although I'm sure he could guess. "I saved our asses. That's all that matters." I wrapped my hands around the cool metal bars, my knuckles whitening. *I don't want to be here. Why did the demon send us here?* A few heartbeats passed as I stared quietly at the house I'd grown up in, the one I'd thought to make my future in as well. Now I never wanted to lay eyes on it again, and yet I couldn't seem to tear them away.

A snarl disrupted the silence, and Makoto slammed Prince Anyon against the gate, his shoulder blades pinging off the thick metal. "You almost got us killed. Who the hell did you piss off that has the kind of power to take out your magic, and kill the Queen of the Light Court?"

The prince slumped his entire body, Makoto's fists the only thing keeping him aloft. "The two aren't connected," he mumbled, his features drooping in utter defeat.

"You need to explain," Makoto grated, lifting and slamming Prince Anyon against the gate again.

I wasn't used to dealing with such a hotheaded Makoto. No matter the form he was in, male or female, he was usually more balanced. I knew why he was off kilter, but it was still jarring, and for that reason, it took me a moment to react.

"Makoto, put him down," I snapped.

His gaze flicked over to meet mine, the irises burning a bright red. "He needs to—"

"You need to put him down." We stared at each other, a few endless moments ticking by before Makoto finally eased away from Prince Anyon, who sank to the ground, head in his hands.

I crouched down beside the prince, scowling. It didn't exactly help that I wanted to throttle him myself. I just had a tad more self-control. "Then tell us what just happened if it wasn't connected to your mother's death."

"It was Crel."

"Crel? Is that name supposed to mean something to us?" I glanced at Makoto, whose eyes had returned to indigo. He shook his head and shrugged.

"Crel is ... or was my lover."

I flopped back on my ass and laughed, the sound dry and without humor. "I should have known. I really should have known." Leave it to Prince Anyon to piss off an ex-lover enough to have that creature want to burn him alive —literally.

"So what'd you do?"

"Crel found me in bed with someone else."

"And that was a surprise?" It was common knowledge that fae were not ... exclusive by nature, and Prince Anyon was probably less so than most. He attempted to lure anyone attractive, male or female, human or magical being, into his bed. His success rate would have been astonishing if not for the fact that he was fae. *Hell, if I hadn't met Makoto, I would have probably found myself in the prince's bed at some point and hated myself for the rest of my existence for it.*

Prince Anyon scrubbed a hand down his face before leaning back against the gate, his head pinging softly against the iron. "He—Crel—well he wanted me to be his *Anam Cara*." He sighed heavily. "I may have led him to believe that I wanted that, too."

"Led him to believe? You mean led him on," Makoto said, coming to stand beside me. I leaned against his legs, finding comfort in just being close to him.

"I love Crel." Prince Anyon slammed his fists against the ground. "I did—or I still do." He lifted his diamond gaze to meet mine, and I knew. I just knew.

"You could have gotten us out of there—"

"But not without hurting Crel," Makoto finished for me.

"Yes."

Makoto flopped down beside me. "Well, I'll be damned. You put someone else's welfare in front of yours —you actually might be in love."

I stared at the prince, utterly stunned. *Out of control fire magic ... Anam Cara ... Wait a second ...* My brain was moving at a snail's pace, what the prince said finally penetrating my consciousness, and I connected the dots to form a very disturbing picture. I jumped to my feet. "Oh my God! Crel is a crazy fire dragon! How the—what the —" I squinted at Prince Anyon, my mind reeling.

Dragon shifters usually didn't intermingle with the rest of us magical beings. It wasn't taboo, or unheard of, it just wasn't common. I didn't know much about their race for that reason, but what I did know was enough for me to want to keep away. You could tell their faction or clan, I wasn't sure what they were actually called, by the color of their hair when in human form. Red hair equaled fire dragon, black hair equaled water dragon, etc. Those were the most powerful of the factions. All dragons could wield fire magic to an extent, but a red dragon ... they were known for their fire and tempers to match, hence why most thought of them as crazy. The red dragons were even more cloistered off than the rest of the dragon factions for that reason. When even your own kind fears you, it's usually a good idea to steer clear. *Apparently, Prince Anyon hadn't gotten the memo.*

"I thought a dragon could only mate with another dragon, or at least a half-breed?" Makoto tugged on one of the braids in his hair. "How could Crel want you for his *Anam Cara?*"

I'd been thinking the same thing. *Anam Cara* was a Celtic term that had been co-opted by humans, much like a lot of things. For a dragon, it meant an unbreakable mate bond, bound by magic, of course. Usually, the bond could only be formed between two dragons, or if one was full-blooded and the other at least part dragon, a hybrid of some sort, it was doable. There was also the little matter of a male dragon being magically able to control the bond. Female dragons had definitely pulled the short straw in the genetic lottery on that one. I wasn't even sure two male dragons could technically form an *Anam Cara* bond, since such magic is linked to genetics and not love. *So how would it work with a male dragon and a male fae?* Sure, Crel might be compelled to bond with Prince Anyon because he loved him, but that didn't mean he'd be able to form the link. Which in my opinion sucked. Love should be able to transcend all boundaries. Unfortunately, it rarely did in reality.

"Could you even actually be his *Anam Cara?*" Makoto asked, again on the same page as me with his line of thought.

"I didn't give Crel a chance to find out," Prince Anyon muttered. "I panicked and seduced another dragon the night before we were going to attempt the claiming."

I scrunched my face. "That's pretty tacky, even for you."

Prince Anyon snorted. "I'm sure Crel would agree."

"Great." Rising, I dusted myself off. "So your mother is dead, murdered by someone unknown, and your crazy ex-dragon-lover is trying to roast you alive. You might actually be in the running with me for most complicated life." *And I'm pretty sure Prince Anyon isn't condemning my relationship with Makoto because of his love of a dragon.* Fae generally looked down their noses at monogamy, let alone with a being that wasn't fae. *Maybe he's not exactly as bad as he seems.* As much as I hated the idea.

But not really. I lifted my head to stare at the manor again, my chest tightening. I knew what I was doing. Sure, I wanted to know who had the power to roast all of us alive, but I didn't actually have the luxury to sit around and discuss such things. I was avoiding having to deal with … everything. As someone who'd lived her entire life coping with things by avoiding her emotions, I knew what was coming would be too much for even me to push aside.

At least with me standing on the front drive of my massacred family's manor. *I need to get out of here.*

"How did they die?" I whispered, unable to resist. I didn't want to know, and yet I needed to.

"Death curse."

I pressed my face against the gate, the bars digging into my cheekbones. "One death curse? I've never heard of such a thing." My voice sounded so small and meek, even to me.

Makoto tugged me into his side, wrapping his arm around my waist. "It was obviously black magic, Rems. It was—"

"Then why had they never attacked us before? It's not like black magic is a new discovery. I just don't—" But I didn't even know if it was the tenebris domos or just some other random black magic wielders. I knew nothing except that they were all dead. Prince Anyon claimed that the tenebris domos had killed off the grey witches, but I had a gut feeling he was just guessing.

I warred with the urge to sink into Makoto's comforting embrace farther or to push him away. I was afraid within the arms of my kitsune I would break down, and I couldn't afford to at the moment either. *Focus. Focus on what you can fix.*

I swiped at an errant tear, internally steeling my will. "There'll be a time for reckoning," I curled my hand over Makoto's heart, "after we fix this." Indigo eyes locked with mine, fear flaring before the emotion could be hidden away. "I promise." I rose onto my tiptoes to deliver a chaste kiss, and he sighed softly against my lips. I inhaled his scent, the unique notes of it fortifying my resolve.

I won't fail you. Not again.

"How anyone thought the two of you were anything less than lovers speaks of the vast stupidity in the witch community."

I growled an obscenity under my breath before turning back to the Prince of Asshats. "So what did you need my help with, *Prince A—*?" I just barely held back from tacking on a colorful name I'm sure he'd make me regret later. Prince Anyon may have been giving me some latitude because of our history, and I wasn't completely powerless against him, but there were certain lines just not worth crossing. I had to pick my battles with someone like him. "And please don't let it be about Crel."

He blinked guileless diamond eyes at me. "Of course it's not about Crel … exactly."

I snorted, my voice dripping with sarcasm, "Color me surprised."

"Mama!"

A feeling of déjà vu washed over me, and I swayed a bit before regaining my footing.

Voo-Dolly scurried out from behind a tree, heading straight for me as fast as her little legs could carry her, her sewn-on smile stretched wide into something akin to a grin. The sun glinted off her one-button eye, and her blue and purple yarn pigtails bounced around her gleeful face.

I dropped to my knees and opened my arms. "Mama!" she cried, leaping at me with joy. The back of my throat burned with emotion as I scooped her up and squeezed her tightly, ignoring the sharp jab of the pins protruding from her body.

"Voo-Dolly!" I pressed my face into the rough burlap that made up her body, inhaling deeply. She felt the same, smelled the same, was the same little voodoo doll that I'd breathed life into by mistake in Somniare. "How are you here?"

Makoto snatched her away from me, scowling, as Voo-Dolly flailed her misshapen arms at him in threat. "Give me back to Mama!"

Ignoring her, Makoto addressed me, "This isn't natural. It was one thing in Somniare, a dreamscape, but here …" His nose scrunched up in disdain. "No. I will not abide by whatever this is. I'm getting rid of it once and for all." His muscles tensed as if he would throw her, and I launched myself at him.

He turned just in time so I ended up hanging off his back. "Don't you dare!" I kicked my legs furiously, banging against the backs of Makoto's knees, trying to throw him off balance. I didn't understand why Makoto hated Voo-Dolly so much, he would never quite say why. It was infuriating. "She's mine! Give me my damn doll!"

Prince Anyon had crept up without my notice, and his arm appeared as if from nowhere, yanking Voo-Dolly away from Makoto lightning-fast.

"Hey!" I cried out, dropping from Makoto. "Give her to me!"

Prince Anyon glided away from me, keeping a few

steps just out of my reach. He cradled Voo-Dolly in his arms, studying her with interest. She lay quiet, doing the same to him. "What is this—this thing?"

"I'm not a thing. I'm Eve." *I forgot I'd let Voo-Dolly rename herself Eve. Oops.*

Prince Anyon nodded slowly. "Okay, Eve. What are you?" He lifted her up into the air and continued to study her at all angles.

"I'm just Eve. And I belong to Mama. She made me." One button eye met mine and my heart clenched.

Eve's presence had once only reminded me of my sister, and now she represented everyone I'd lost. *But is she really the same doll? Or do you just want to believe she is?* Because this time I didn't give her life, Kiernan had. That in itself made her different. And maybe there were a few other things that gave me pause. *Is her button eye on the opposite side now? And what about her heart, that looks a bit off too.* The more I inspected her, I realized she wasn't physically identical to the doll from Somniare. *But she feels the same. That's all that matters. After all, I don't look the same anymore either.*

Kiernan's words echoed in my head.

"I'm going to send a gift to you. Don't question it. Use it."

"Remember, like magic calls to like magic. Use mine to find my body."

I waved my hand in the air, nonchalantly using a sensing spell. I nodded to myself, having confirmed what I'd suspected when the feel of wild magic hummed along my skin, strong and familiar. Kiernan had sent me Eve, filled to the brim with his magic as a way to aid me in finding his body. His magic that lived within me probably wasn't enough to get the job done, or maybe he just wanted insurance of some sort. He'd chosen wisely to make sure I'd keep his 'gift' close to me. Not that I had a choice. If I wanted to save Makoto, I had to play along with Kiernan until I could seize the opportunity for my revenge.

Watching the prince trying to figure out Eve triggered the memory of one other thing Kiernan had said.

"Do not reveal my existence to Prince Anyon."

Again, not that I'd been planning on divulging any details about Kiernan to the prince, but I also had to remember to be extra careful. I couldn't give Kiernan any excuses to do something to punish me by way of Makoto.

"Give her to me," I grated, magic sparking in my palms. "There's nothing to know about her beyond the fact that I created her."

Prince Anyon tilted his head, shifting his inquisitive gaze to me. "But why?"

"She made the original when she was a child. It reminds Rems of her sister," Makoto offered. "But feel free to dispose of it. It's unnatural here in this world."

"Traitor," I hissed. "You never liked her, even in Somniare."

Prince Anyon chuckled, setting Eve down on her feet. She yanked a pin from her arm, stabbing the prince in the leg, before dancing nimbly away.

"Ow, why you little—" He snatched at her, glowering.

Eve flew at me, her expression somehow smug, and I scooped her up, burying my face where one of her ears would be. "Don't tell him anything. Don't trust him," I whispered on an exhale of breath. She nodded subtly, burlap scratching against my skin.

"I can hear you," Prince Anyon snapped. "And I thought we were friends."

I raised my head, shifting Eve to my hip. "We've never been friends, and we both know it."

The prince leaned against the gate, his features pinched. "You know, witches and humans are more alike than you think. At least when it comes to your emotions. We are friends, Remy."

I rolled my eyes. "Uh-huh. We'll just have to agree to disagree."

"What do you want our help with?" Makoto prodded.

"Crel has something of mine, and I need you to get it back."

"You want us to get something back from the dragon who just tried to fry all of us alive?" Makoto stalked forward, the fingers on his left hand swirling through the air as if he was imagining holding Tarik. "I just saved Rems from death, and I don't want to have to do it again."

Makoto was dangerously close to revealing what had really sent us to Somniare—my murder, and my status of being quasi-dead while there. Somehow Prince Anyon hadn't been surprised, or maybe hadn't cared, that I even possessed the power to go to the dream landscape. It'd been a secret from everyone except for those closest to me. I didn't want the prince to know that we'd used blood magic to restore my life-force completely, because that would lead directly to Kiernan eventually. *I need to change the subject quick.*

As if on cue, a distraction presented itself.

"Remy, baby," my sister's voice lilted softly.

I whipped my head around, my knees wobbling. On the other side of the gate was a transparent image of Callie. It flickered and rippled like she was underwater. *Is she a ghost? Or a hallucination of some sort?*

"I need to show you something." She turned, her dark hair flowing behind her as she ran towards the house.

I need to know. I scrambled to follow, even though I didn't get very far.

Makoto's fingers dug into my forearm, yanking me to the side. "Don't follow it … whatever it is. It's not your sister. You know that."

"I don't know that! You didn't even try to sense her!" I tore away from him. "And I don't know anything either! I need to find out!"

I threw out my hands, a ball of raw magic smashing into the gate and opening it, the clang of metal hitting metal reverberating through my head.

"Callie, wait!" I sprinted after my sister's image, tripping over my long skirt. "Damnit! This thing needs to go once and for all."

I waved my hands down my body, calling forth a simple spell, and yet one I'd never actually used before.

My skin tingled as dark jeans, black boots, and a black tank top replaced the blue dress.

"Tarik," I murmured, "I'm gonna need you, too." The katana blinked into existence, blazing a bright white, humming with anticipation.

I didn't know what I was about to walk into, but I felt a bit more prepared having finally shed the restrictive dress from the night of my murder, and of course, with the power of Tarik buzzing through my system.

"Let's do this."

Chapter 6

As always, Tarik affected my emotions. With him blazing the way through the shadows of oncoming dusk, while held tightly in my hand, I felt invincible. I didn't even mind that he hadn't brought his magical armor for me. *That's because we don't need it. Tarik knows what's up.*

I registered on some level that Makoto was giving me chase, probably in fox form, but I wasn't stopping until I had answers. Landmines were waiting to blow up in my face if I took a wrong step when it came to so many things … too many things. The clearer my path, the better it would be.

I raced into the manor, the heavy wooden door at the main entrance hanging off its hinges. It was dark in the house, eerily so. It was as if the ebbing light from the day didn't even dare enter the space, and yet there I was, boldly giving chase to Callie … my dead sister. *If I didn't have Tarik I wouldn't be so confident.* Sometimes being cautious is a good thing, I knew that to be true, but I couldn't remember why, at least not under Tarik's influence.

"Callie," I called.

"This way." My sister's translucent form hovered at the top of the grand staircase.

"Rems, don't."

Ignoring Makoto, I rushed forward, Tarik shifting to an indigo shade as we ascended the steps. My heart thundered in my ears, anticipation and excitement pinging through my system.

In between one step and the next, colors and sounds exploded around me, as if someone had flicked a light switch of life on in the house. I stumbled forward, grabbing onto the railing with one hand to steady myself.

"Remy," Callie's voice caressed my ear, "pay attention."

I forced myself to finish climbing the staircase, confusion replacing the excitement I'd been feeling moments before. A soft instrumental jazz tune filled the air, the notes distorted as if I was listening to them from underwater.

Callie's arms wrapped around me, surrounding me in warmth and comfort. "Oh, Remy baby, you're so grown up." She kept hold of my hands as she moved back to look at me. "I hate that I'm going to miss seeing all the things that get you here—to be the person you are today."

"What is this? Are you a ghost?"

She smiled, her eyes submerged in sadness. "This is a spell. I'm communicating with you from the past."

"B-but how ... why?" *Why* was definitely a better question. The *how* was obviously magic. Such spells that allowed a witch to make contact with other witches through the fabric of time were difficult, but not unheard of. It simply expended a lot of energy, and in the end, usually changed nothing. So why was my sister using up valuable energy to contact me from the past, and why now?

"I've seen the future." Groaning, she shook her head. "I've seen so much ... too much. And I know there isn't anything I can do about most of it, not even my own death, but I can help you," she tucked a piece of my hair behind my ear, "my baby sister."

"You know you're going to be murdered?" I croaked. "And you couldn't—"

"No. Please don't ask me about that. We have little time, and there are things I have to show you."

The scenery around us changed, and I moved forward, squinting. "What is—"

"Shhh ... just watch," Callie commanded.

Another Callie, or Callie in yet another timeline ran past us. She wore faded jeans and a black tank top, her feet bare. Instant recognition jolted me. It's what she'd been wearing the night she'd been murdered.

"You know this is inevitable. You've seen it and accepted it. Why do you run?" a male voice called from the shadows.

Without a word, the Callie in jeans and a tank top pushed into the manor, her bare feet slapping against the wood floors. I already knew where she was going ... to the place her body would be found.

I waited to follow Callie, wanting to see who stalked her, the voice familiar, even if the callous tone was not. When my eyes alighted on him ... My hand fluttered to my throat, my stomach churning with bile. *It can't be. There's no way. It just—*

But it was. The man emerging from the dark—the man who would kill my sister—stab her too many times to count while she'd been bound by magic to not fight back, to endure the pain until her blood stained the floors and her life-force leaked from her body ... was our father. Our father was the one who had murdered Callie.

"No," I hissed. "It can't be. It has to be a spell. A shapeshifting spell or ... or something else. I don't know, but it wasn't him. It ..." But hadn't our mother been the one to stab me the night of my ascension ceremony? I'd been seventeen years old, just like Callie. I knew there'd been a connection, but I'd never considered ... I shook my head. I guess I was still holding out hope that my mother had attempted to kill me for a good reason. Like she'd had a vision and knew I'd survive the attack on Domus Novem only if I was in Somniare.

Numbly, I stumbled into the house, following my father. He moved slowly, his steps deliberate, like he had all the time in the world to track down and murder my sister, and maybe he did. No one had ever been able to figure out how Callie had been killed within the manor without anyone sensing or seeing anything. We were a house full of powerful witches, and it was as if she'd been murdered by a phantom. Because of the uncertainty, and yes, fear, her death had been swept under the rug, no one wanting to deal with the possibility that one of our own had done it.

A part of me still didn't accept it, but I knew it was him —my father, and not a spell. His DNA coursed through me, making my magic recognize his. There were no spells that could mask or hide close family ties from a witch like me. I'd been trained as the next Grand Witch to recognize such things instantly, my senses honed to them.

Down the long hallway, and past achingly familiar things, I trailed along behind my father, a man I'd trusted, a man who had helped raise me ... *Why? Why would he kill her and then mourn with the rest of us?*

Callie froze in front of her open door, her room—her sanctuary. She'd probably headed there on instinct, not knowing what else to do. "Dad! Why? Why are you doing this?" Tears tracked down her cheeks as my father twisted his hand, spinning her in the air. "I saw what you would do, but I can't understand why!"

"You know why. It's nothing personal, baby."

"Nothing personal?" she squeaked. "I'm your daughter! Your flesh and blood!"

"And that's why your power belongs to me! You wouldn't even exist if I hadn't created you!"

My body was fraught with tension, taut. I was viewing

something that had already happened, the past, and I knew I couldn't change it. But I needed to do more than I needed to draw my next breath.

I raised Tarik, fire creeping from my palms up the blade, sparks raining down on me. "Aaaaah!" I screamed, through gritted teeth. I sprinted, my legs pumping hard, and when I reached my father I stabbed, sliced, and jabbed, anger causing me to mutter violent, nonsensical things. But I might as well have been attacking a shadow because Tarik's blade passed through him without delivering any damage.

I dropped to my knees and screamed again, Callie's voice pitching high in pain to match mine. *I can't look. I don't want to see.* But I had to. I was brought to the scene of my sister's murder for a reason. Callie needed me to see it. My fingers loosened, Tarik slipping from my grip, disappearing before he hit the floor.

I lifted my gaze just as my father released his magic, and Callie's body dropped to the ground with a sickening thud. She moaned, still alive, holding on by a thread. Blood dribbled from what seemed like a thousand tiny holes in her flesh, pooling under her crumpled form. I'd always known that the way she died wouldn't have been fast, or painless, but I never let my mind go there. Now I had no choice. I choked back a sob, hating how helpless I felt. *What good is knowledge if you can't do anything with it?*

My father crouched over Callie's still form, sweeping a tendril of dark hair from her forehead. "It's almost over, I promise." His voice was tender, soft. "I'm sorry you have to die for me to take it. I wish it didn't have to be this way. I know you probably don't believe that, but I do—mean it."

He stood abruptly, his visage darkening. My translation rune burned as he muttered the words I'd learned to fear, words that warlocks used to steal a witch's magic. "What's yours is now mine, for all of time." The spell was nothing more than a focusing tool, acknowledging the intent of the warlock to actually take the magic from a witch. Those words were merely there to serve as a safeguard from errant thoughts of jealousy.

Callie bucked up, her back arching, and her mouth opening in a silent scream. Silver and black waves of power slithered from her into my father. "No," he hissed, even as he continued siphoning all of my sister's magic, killing her completely. "Where is it? What did you do with it?"

My sister laughed, blood bubbling up from her lips and dribbling down her cheeks. "Like you said, I knew you'd kill me ... had accepted it. But I couldn't let you ... have ..." Her eyes dimmed, and her last breath stuck in her chest.

"No." My father dropped down beside her, his open palm slamming into her sternum. "What did you do with it? Tell me!" But she was dead, and no more answers would be coming from her.

After staring into Callie's lifeless eyes for a few heartbeats, my father uncurled himself to stand tall. "No matter," he mumbled. "I'll find it. There are only so many things you could have done with it."

The scene wavered, and I found myself standing beside the translucent figure of my sister. I reached out to her, wanting to touch her again, but her magic was weakening, the spell coming to an end soon. "God, Callie, how do you deal with knowing that's how you'll die?" And how odd was it that to the Callie communicating with me, it hadn't happened to her yet.

"I needed you to know about him."

"How did you know to come to me now—now of all times?"

She smiled. "You know that the best spells are when the magic guides you. I let it decide. It knew what to do."

"So all of this was just to let me know about our father? But he's already dead. All of Domus Novem was slaughtered."

"He's not dead." She waved her hand and an image of our father in a black robe appeared in front of us. He raised his hood and—

"He's the warlock from Somniare? But how is that possible? How didn't I sense him? How could I have not known?"

"That doesn't matter. What does is that he's figured out I gave you what he wants. That's why he wasn't interested in you one way or the other at first, and then he realized— he tasted it. He tasted the magic, and he'll stop at nothing to get it. He's the one who led the warlocks here," she waved her hand around, motioning to the manor, "to kill our domos. He was still looking for what I hid—he'd discovered that I put it in another witch."

"But wait—" I struggled to remember Somniare clearly. The longer I was out of the dreamscape, the more certain pieces faded away like I'd actually been dreaming. "There was more than one warlock. First, there was Jared, and I killed him. Then there was—"

"He has control of them. All of them. He's linked to them as if he's their master—their puppet master."

Confusion about absolutely everything crashed into me, threatening to drown me. *Is anything I thought true? Or has my entire life been one big lie?* And why hadn't Callie told me what would happen before she was murdered? I might have been just a child, but there had to have been a better way for both of us.

Before I could say anything in response, Callie raised her hand to silence me. "You need to know what you're up against, and you need to learn to how to control my power, and fast. You have to keep it hidden like before."

I didn't understand, and I was rapidly beginning to suspect I never would. I mean, why give me this power if I was supposed to hide it? Why not destroy it to keep it from my father, and keep me safe? "What is it? What's this mysterious power?"

Every witch had a specialty, or an area of magic that they were more gifted in than the others. Every witch except a Grand Witch, that is. Grand Witches were talented in all areas, which was why we rose within the ranks in our domos. Sometimes, like in my case, the power was sensed right away, while others had to mature before their destiny was uncovered. *So why, if I was the powerful one, had my father been after Callie's gift?*

"Necromancy. My talent is necromancy."

I reeled, and unbidden a memory from Somniare rose up within my mind.

My gaze tracked down to my sister's lifeless body lying crumpled at my feet, her expression vacant and dull. In her arms was my voodoo doll. I dropped to my knees, soundless sobs escaping my chest.

"You can save her." The words slithered around me, seducing my will.

"I don't know how to do that kind of magic. I'm not a necromancer."

"You know how."

Yes. I do know how. It would be easy. So easy.

I lifted my hands to hover over my sister's chest. "Live," I demanded, my magic infusing with my words. "Live!"

I swayed, nausea roiling my gut. "No. That power was bound. It doesn't come to witches anymore, at least not naturally." Was that vision in Somniare another thing that was actually true? Did the power of necromancy live within me without my conscious knowledge?

"I don't know how or why, Remy. I just know I have the gift of necromancy and our father wanted it for himself."

I wanted to laugh.

I wanted to cry.

I wanted to punch something—kill something—*do* something. I hated feeling so lost and powerless.

Instead, I did what I always did: donned cold indifference to get me through it.

I rubbed my temples. Kiernan and Callie both had given me magic. How much of my power was even my own anymore? "So what'd he want it for? And why didn't you simply destroy it? Wouldn't that have been the best option?"

Callie's eyebrows rose to her hairline. "An army. He wants to raise an undead army. Or at least that's what I think. That part I don't know for sure. And I can't destroy it—I don't know how. The magic is different. I couldn't risk telling anyone, so much more would have been at risk."

"Oh, an undead army, is that all?" I deadpanned.

"Remy." My sister hunched forward, her hair falling into her face, a dark curtain blocking her expression from my view. "I'm sorry. I wish I could do more than warn you. I wish I could be there for you. I'm afraid what I'm going to do, or did from your perspective, is only going to cause more trouble. I was just trying to—there are things beyond us—things I saw that go way beyond just us. There was ever only one choice for me."

"It's fine. I understand." My throat tightened, my eyes burning. Despite my best efforts, it was difficult to ignore the emotions that swirled within me. I was talking to my sister. Actually talking to her. It didn't matter that we were doing it across the fabric of time. "I've missed you," I choked out, regretting the words.

I was met by silence. My sister had disappeared. I swore I could smell the flowery body spray she used to wear. Tarik slipped from my grasp and disappeared before he hit the floor, me having called him again without consciously realizing it.

"Rems!" Makoto's furry fox body slammed into mine, taking me to the ground. "Where were you? I couldn't see you but I could scent you." A flash of purple revealed Makoto's original male form. "I thought—I didn't know what to think." He crushed me to his chest, his heart galloping.

I wrapped my arms around him, burying my face in his kimono. His presence steadied me, grounding me in a way only Makoto could. "It was my sister. She contacted me from the past."

"What did she tell you? It must have been important." His fingers crept down my spine, as if he was checking to see if I was still all in one piece.

"My father murdered her. He murdered Callie."

Makoto's embrace tightened around me, his body saying the only words I needed. He was here for me, no matter what. "We have a lot to talk about. A lot of new things to consider."

Callie had been murdered by my father at seventeen, which was the age most female witches were at their most powerful, and most vulnerable, a rare combination that only happened naturally to a witch, once in a lifetime.

Somewhere between our seventeenth and eighteenth year was when witches ascended to our full powers, which makes stealing them more difficult. So why did my mom murder me right before my ascension? Neither she nor my father had attempted to steal my powers, or I wouldn't have been able to get to Somniare. *What am I missing? I still don't have so many pieces to the puzzle.* I had to find out.

I pulled away from Makoto. "Where is Prince Anyon?"

Makoto shrugged. "Somewhere around here. Who really cares?"

"What about Eve?"

"I'm here, Mama!" Eve waddled out from the shadows, waving enthusiastically.

"Great," Makoto muttered. "I thought I lost her."

Ignoring his ever-present disdain for my voodoo doll, I pressed on. "I need to summon my mother's spirit. I need to talk to her." I raked my hands through my knotted hair, grimacing when I tore at a snarl. "And I need to do it before his stupid royal fae-ness shows up."

Lines of worry creased Makoto's forehead. "Summon her spirit? But—"

"I don't have a choice. This could very well be life or death. I promise I'll explain absolutely everything ... after."

"All right. I'll gather what you need." Makoto transformed back into the fox, the purple flash causing spots to dance in front of my eyes.

I pinched the bridge of my nose, blinking rapidly. "Makoto, please hurry." In a blur of motion, my kitsune zoomed off.

"Come here, Eve." I opened my arms to my doll, smothering her against my chest as soon as she was close enough for me to touch.

"Why, Callie?" I clutched the stuffed voodoo doll in my arms. I'd labored for hours over it, my small fingers sore and bleeding from my efforts. "Is something wrong?"

"Just give me the doll, Remy."

I clutched it tighter, shaking my head. "I made it all by myself. I wanted to use her for—"

My sister snatched the doll from me with ease; my small arms no match for her. "Callie!" I snapped, indignant. "That's mine, give it back. Now."

Her expression softened as she studied my face and then the doll. "Remy, baby, why did you give it a smile ... and a heart?"

I shrugged, suddenly embarrassed. But I knew my sister wouldn't let it go until she got an answer. She'd always been more like a second mother to me than an older sibling. "I wanted to practice doing love spells."

She laughed. "Love spells? With a voodoo doll? Remy, baby, that's not what a voodoo doll is for. And Novems don't do love spells."

My lower lip quivered, my cheeks heating with shame. I hated feeling stupid. "What's a voodoo doll for then? And why don't we do love spells?"

Ignoring my questions, my sister handed me back the doll. "Here. You can keep it, as long as you don't practice magic on it. Especially love spells." Her gaze slid over the doll once more, her lips twitching. "It's kind of cute, but don't tell anyone I said that."

"I don't want it anymore." I hurled the doll at the ground, tears dripping from my lashes.

Now more than ever, I wanted to keep Eve next to me. She was not only associated with my last childhood memory of Callie, but now it somehow felt like she was the last tie to my family that I had left.

"It's okay, Mama. We'll get everything sorted out."

As I held my living voodoo doll, cradling her like a small child, an errant thought passed through my mind. *Everything is connected. Callie's death, Kiernan, my father, my murder, my mother ... everything.* I just needed to figure out how exactly, and fast.

Chapter 7

My hands shook as I placed the white candles on the ground, forming a small circle. In the center, with a grease pencil, I carefully drew the Novem symbol with the addition of my spell signature, which was nothing more than a fancy R woven into the original pattern. Then I placed the picture of my mother that Makoto had snagged from some old family photo album in the center of the circle. The photo wasn't necessary, a piece of hair, or any object that had belonged to my mother would have done, but the picture would be the easiest for me to use since I'd only conjured spirits when I'd been in training, and then, I just called forth any available entity.

I stood, wiping my brow with the back of my hand. "Fire," I murmured, lighting all the candles simultaneously.

Makoto grabbed my hand, intertwining our fingers. "I'm here."

I loved that he didn't tell me not to do the spell, or say some other kind of bullshit, like it'll be okay, or something like that. His simple words of 'I'm here' were exactly what I needed. No matter what happened, how bad things got, I could always count on Makoto to be there for me. "Yeah, I know."

He dropped my hand and stepped back, giving me the room I needed to work. "Remember to stay focused. Don't let your mind wander."

I bit the inside of my cheek, tasting blood. *He had to go and ruin the moment, didn't he?* "That happened one time. One. Time. And it was my first summoning. It hasn't happened since then."

The first time I'd conjured a spirit, my mind had wandered somewhere in the middle of the spell, and I'd ended up calling forth a dog's spirit. I'd been thinking of puppies or something and the next thing I knew, Cujo was harassing me from the otherworld. It had traumatized me at the time, especially since I was only thirteen, and I'd been afraid to attempt the spell again for some time.

"Okay. I just want to make sure you're fully focused. We don't have time to deal with random spirits."

"I'm focused."

"Okay, then. So go ahead and start the spell."

"I don't need your permission," I growled. "I'll start when I start."

Silence engulfed us, Makoto obviously biting his own

tongue to keep from saying anything else. That was the thing about him having grown up with me … sometimes it felt like my kitsune knew entirely too much about me. It was something I loved, and yet hated at the same time. *I guess that's just the way it always is with romantic relationships that bloom between best friends.*

I flicked my gaze down to my mother's picture, the glossy finish dancing with the light of the flames. *She looks happy.* My mother was smiling, waving her hand in front of her face as if to block the camera. *Did my father take it? Had anything ever been real between them? Between any of us as a family?*

I pushed those thoughts aside, focusing on my mother's features, staring into her dark eyes. *Come forth from the beyond. Share with me your knowledge. Come forth from the beyond …* I repeated the words in my mind, over and over, until they blended together, perpetuating themselves. Every witch used different words for their spells, it was a myth that things had to be done just so. It was more about learning how to focus and use one's own magic properly. It was only the darker arts that required special knowledge beyond what a witch was born with.

"Remy," my mother's voice whispered, a moment before her spirit stepped into the circle of candles. "What … why—oh." Confusion had played across her features before the awareness of what was going on settled over her. "I suppose you want answers."

I hadn't planned on being combative, but before I could stop myself, the words spilled from my mouth,

"Why did you murder me?" My tone was sharp, accusatory.

She pursed her lips, her gaze darting around. "Death would come prematurely for all of us in Domus Novem, even you, there was no way around that, but you would be the only one who actually had a loophole—who came back."

Relief caused me to sag. Deep down, I'd still been holding onto hope that my mother had murdered me to protect me. "You made sure I was in Somniare ..."

"Yes, you would have been slaughtered with the rest of us if I hadn't forced Makoto's hand." Her gaze met mine with knowing. "You may have thought I wasn't a good mother to you, cold sometimes." She laughed darkly. "Okay, most of the time, but I hadn't just lost Callie that night, I'd lost the man I loved," her voice grew thick with emotion, "and I had to pretend I didn't know anything, so I could protect you."

For the first time since Callie's death I understood, truly understood my mother. "I forgive you."

She sobbed, hunching over as she wound her arms around her middle. She looked so small, so vulnerable, and I couldn't believe I'd never seen this side of her before. *I've been blind.* Either that or my mother deserved a damn Academy Award for her performance over the years.

"Tell me about Callie's gift. About the necromancy. Hell, tell me anything you know about my father, my magic—anything."

"The gift of sight can be a blessing and a curse. Be glad you didn't get it like Callie and I both did. It only shows so much. Possible outcomes, one specific event, sometimes it's just a flash, and others more vivid." She straightened. "I was shown that there was no way for the rest of us to escape death, and the only slim chance for you was in Somniare. That's all I know."

It made sense. If my mother hadn't murdered me on the night of my ascension ceremony, then Makoto wouldn't have panicked and sought out Kiernan to make the deal that resulted in saving my life. My personal timeline had been irrevocably altered by my mother's actions. But in order for her to know about my power to go to Somniare, then it already happened, and that would mean—

I groaned, rubbing my temples. Time travel hurt my head. Because that's what Kiernan had done. He'd gone back in Somniare to when I'd been a child to begin feeding me his magic so when my mother struck, I'd have the ability to save myself. The problem was, Makoto hadn't brokered the deal until I'd already been stabbed. *It's all so friggin' complicated.* Not for the first time, I realized I wasn't going to make sense out of those things. I simply had to accept what was and move on.

"What about our father? Can you tell me anything else about him?"

"No. Well …" Her dark gaze captured mine, imploring. "I want you to know that he was a good man once. And then something changed him." She shook her head slowly.

"I doubt we'll ever know what though. But he loved me, and you ... and Callie."

My mind flashed to him plunging a blade repeatedly into my sister's body, and I shuddered. I wasn't sure I could ever believe that again, but I didn't want to antagonize my mother's spirit. "Yeah, okay," I mumbled. "I need to know about the necromancy. How did—"

My mother spun within the circle. "Something's coming!"

The words were barely out of her mouth when the flames from the candles shot up into the air, before fizzling out. My heart quadrupled in time, the sudden darkness getting to me. "Mom?"

The candles rekindled, fresh flames burning brighter than before. A massive male silhouette stood in the circle where my mother's spirit had been a moment ago.

"What is the meaning of this?" he roared.

Before I could react, I was flung through the air, slamming into the wall. A picture frame slid off the wall, crashing to the ground next to me.

"Mama!" Eve was next to me instantly, wielding a pin in each of her hands, as if she could ward off any other attacks.

"How dare you!" Makoto shot across the floor, surrounded by a vibrant blue-purple flame. He threw out his hands, and spheres of the fire rocketed towards the silhouette.

I clapped a hand over my mouth, utter astonishment dominating every other emotion running rapidly through me. "Fox-fire," I choked out. Up until that very moment, Makoto had never been able to call upon his fox-fire. It was something that all kitsunes developed, but usually not until they got their fourth or fifth tail. Makoto had sacrificed his fourth tail to Kiernan to save my life, and so the appearance of his fox-fire was shocking.

"You'll wish you were dead for trying to hurt her!" Makoto's ball o' flames were met by a wall of fire produced by our unknown visitor, but that didn't deter my kitsune. He rose up into the air, his fox-fire crackling like it was supercharged with electricity. This time, dual jets of flame exploded from Makoto's hands, pummeling against the wall of fire.

The wall merely grew and expanded, as if Makoto's fox-fire was feeding it. "Fire, even fox-fire can't get past my defenses," the silhouette proclaimed with a laugh. "For I am dragon."

A dragon, here? Oh. "Crel?" I called. "Are you Crel?"

I was met with silence, before, "Who are you?"

I pulled myself to my feet, calling forth some healing to fix the small bump on the back of my head. "Makoto, stop. It's Crel. And I'm fine. I must have messed up the spell. He's probably confused about how he turned up in my circle."

"I don't care how or why he showed up in your circle," Makoto hissed. "He tried to hurt you." Eve danced around, waving her pins as if in agreement.

I moved forward cautiously, one tentative footstep at a time. When I was close enough, I reached out towards the fox-fire surrounding my kitsune, wiggling my fingers. "Turn it off, or you'll burn me."

"No. I'm going to punish him for what he did to you."

I glanced up to study Makoto's profile. His jaw muscles were popping with tension, and his eyebrows were pulled low on his forehead, drawing attention to his red eyes. I had no doubt his anger, his very over-the-top anger, was brought on by the imbalance in him. His mood swings were getting worse. I needed to bring him back under control.

My hand trembled slightly, but I was determined to call Makoto's bluff. Or maybe I wouldn't, maybe I'd find out what it felt like to be burned by fox-fire. "Makoto, turn it off." I was a hairsbreadth away from making contact.

He didn't even turn in my direction as he continued shooting fox-fire. I gritted my teeth, squeezed my eyes shut, and shoved my hand forward, prepared for the worst.

No pain came. I opened one eye, halfway, and peeked. The fox-fire was still blazing bright, and my hand was indeed in the fire, but it wasn't harming me at all. *Duh. Of course it wouldn't, Makoto's my familiar. Just like my flames can't hurt him, his can't hurt me.* And he'd known the whole time, essentially making my move to call his bluff pointless.

But that little detail also reminded me of something else. "Makoto. Don't make me do it. Don't make me bend your will to mine. You're still my familiar, remember?"

He turned slowly, his fierce expression hardening. "You wouldn't do that to me." His nostrils flared as he struggled to breathe evenly. "You would never do that to me."

I quirked an eyebrow in challenge. "Wouldn't I? You're unbalanced. You'd forgive me … eventually."

"He tried to hurt you. Let me punish him. I need to make him pay."

"No, Makoto. It's not something you'd normally want. The imbalance is getting worse." When his eyes narrowed, I decided to use a different tactic. "Please, Makoto. I can't lose you. This," I motioned at the fox-fire streaming steadily in Crel's direction, "isn't you. I'm afraid. I'm afraid of you."

The fox-fire popped out of existence and the next moment I found myself wrapped in Makoto's tight embrace. He pressed his chin to the top of my head, inhaling deeply. "I never want you to be afraid of me. Never."

"What the hell is he doing here?" Prince Anyon's voice sounded from behind us.

The sensation of falling washed over me, and when I opened my eyes, pulling away from Makoto to get a look around, I realized the three of us, plus Eve, were standing in the center of a strange room. It was massive, so large that I couldn't see the end of it. And white, it was astoundingly white, as if dirt was afraid to exist. Realization donned on me.

"We're in Alternum." I glared at Prince Anyon. "Why did you bring us here?"

The prince, looking more flustered than I ever imagined a fae of his status could appear, glared right back at me. "Crel was there. What the hell was Crel doing there?"

I laughed. "You panicked, didn't you?"

"I don't panic, I made a quick strategic decision."

Makoto met my gaze, smirking. "He totally panicked."

"Mama!" Eve said, her tiny body moving up and down on Prince Anyon's super-sized bed, her grin stretched wide as she sailed up into the air over and over again. "This is the realm we need to be in. I can feel it."

Kiernan's body was in Alternum? *Crappity, crap, crap, crap. Does it always have to be the hard way for me?* Hoping to change the subject before the prince started asking questions, I brought up the one thing guaranteed to distract. "Why didn't you just talk to him?"

"Crel?" Prince Anyon squeaked. "No. I'd rather not."

"But you still love him," I said.

"It makes no difference if I do. Crel is insane. I can't reason with him."

"Hmm ... yeah, well, I'm pretty sure if I caught Rems in bed with someone else the night before we were supposed to attempt a mate bond, I might lose my mind, too," Makoto stated.

Prince Anyon waved him off. "It's different. Kitsunes mate for life and are monogamous by nature. It's different for fae."

"You shouldn't have led Crel on then," Makoto growled. "You have no one to blame but yourself for …"

I tuned out the rest of the conversation. My mind had already moved on to tracking down Kiernan's body. Once we got Makoto's spirit heart back, it'd be much easier to deal with the rest of the stuff on our plate. I'd thought getting out of Somniare would be the most difficult part, but it turned out to be just the beginning.

"Rems." Makoto snapped his fingers in front of my face. "Did you hear any of that?"

"Yeah, of course."

His face twisted with skepticism. "Then what did Prince Anyon just say?"

"Something about Crel?"

"No. He said—"

"I need you to get back a very strong charm that Crel stole from me," Prince Anyon interjected.

I crossed my arms over my chest. "And why would I do that? Why should I care about some charm?"

"It's a fae charm."

I rolled my eyes. "Oh. My bad … why should I care about some fae charm?" *I need to get out of here so we can find Kiernan's body.*

"Rems." Makoto cupped my cheek, turning me to face him. "It's one of *the* fae charms." He quirked an eyebrow with meaning.

I blinked several times, processing. "You're kidding?" I turned to glare at the prince. "You're both kidding, right?"

Prince Anyon scowled. "I'd never joke about such a thing."

"Which one? Which one does Crel have?"

"The one that amps up powers."

The fae charms were each as old as the fae themselves, or so it was thought. No one actually knew the origins of the charms. Some thought they didn't exist at all. Because of that, they had no real names and were merely referred to vaguely, if at all. But I believed all of them were real. I'd come to find over my short lifespan that the kind of rumors that just won't die, usually aren't rumors at all.

"Oh," was all I could manage. It wasn't the worst charm Crel could have gotten his hands on, definitely not the deadliest by far, at least not in itself. I knew from lore, never actually confirmed until moments ago, that the Light Court had such an object to make sure the king or queen, stayed the king or queen. It gave the bearer an added boost of power in case anyone magically challenged them. The real question was: how the hell had Crel gotten his hands on it?

Makoto sat on the edge of the bed and perched his chin in his hands. "But even though he's pissed, he still loves you. You need to fix it. Talk to him."

"How did you pull him into your circle?" Prince Anyon blurted. "None of that makes sense."

"And Makoto had his fox-fire ..." I slapped my palm into my forehead. "Duh. Crel had the charm on him. It affected all of our powers."

Prince Anyon shifted to lounge across a white couch,

stretching his long legs out languidly. "That's not how it works. The charm—"

"You know what? I don't really care about the charm. It's fae politics and has nothing to do with us. What, or rather who would you have turned to if you hadn't stumbled across Makoto and me outside that hospital? You can't tell me you were just hiding here in Alternum, hoping something would go your way."

The prince stared at me, his lips thinning, telling me everything I needed to know. His mother had been murdered, the fae charm stolen, and the brat prince had been waiting around for someone else to do his dirty work. *Well, it's not going to be me.*

"What about the war?"

I padded over to sit next to Makoto. "I'm not so sure the war is coming, like you say. I think you're attempting to use scare tactics to motivate us to help you. Domos magicaes have been wiped out before. Tears in the fabric between realities have existed …" I popped to my feet. "And it was all sorted out in the end. I don't really see the connection between any of that and your charm."

"Rems." Makoto tugged me back down next to him. "If that charm falls into the wrong hands it could be devastating for all of us—for the world. It doesn't matter if the war is coming or not, that charm in the wrong hands, could bring about a lot of destruction. The world as everyone knows it could come to an end."

I grabbed the sides of Makoto's face, leaning into him.

"You are my world. I don't care what happens to anyone or anything else."

He opened and shut his mouth, but no sound escaped. Instead, he pressed his lips to mine fiercely, using his touch to communicate what he couldn't put into words. His tongue swept into my mouth, twining with mine. But before I could sink into the kiss—sink into him—he broke away from me. "I care about the rest of the world, Rems. It matters to me."

I turned away from him and cursed under my breath. Even unbalanced, hurtling towards the kind of darkness that would consume his kitsune soul, Makoto was still worried about more than himself. He cared what happened to the world. I'd thought Somniare had changed me, and maybe it had in some small ways, but in the end, I was still mostly concerned with only Makoto and myself. I wouldn't care if the entire world burned, just as long as the two of us were okay.

"I still don't understand why his royal pain in the ass doesn't just use his magic to snag the damn charm back. He—" I turned to glare at the prince. "You know exactly where it is. So what if your ex-lover has it."

"The charm can't be sensed by fae."

"Again, so what? You know Crel has it ..." I raised my eyebrows. "Go and get it. This isn't our problem. None of it is. Stop being an entitled fae asshat and go grovel to Crel. I bet if you beg, maybe crawl around in the dirt like the pig you are, he might give you the charm back. Why don't you try scaring him with the threat of the big bad war? Maybe that con will work on him. After all, he fell for your lies before."

My stomach rumbled loudly, and I stumbled forward when I tried to stand. A wave of dizziness caused my vision to blur. I staggered a few steps before finally pitching forward. Makoto caught me before the floor could meet my face, thankfully.

"Food. I completely forgot about food. And thirsty. I'm so thirsty." I swallowed convulsively, my mouth devoid of moisture. I hadn't needed to eat or drink in Somniare, and with all the craziness and confusion since finding our way back to reality, I'd forgotten about that little bodily necessity. It was strange how I hadn't been hungry or thirsty until that very moment. Maybe my body was still adjusting. It was the only thing that made sense.

Makoto placed me gently on Prince Anyon's bed and pulled a blanket over me. "Rest, Rems. I'll get you what you need."

I attempted to protest, but my body had no energy to fight. My eyes fluttered shut in submission, and I was asleep almost instantly.

Chapter 8

Thump-thump, thump-thump, thump-thump ...

"Am I to assume that I'm going to see you every time I fall asleep or am knocked unconscious now?"

"It's the only time I have to communicate with you," Kiernan rumbled.

"I need to invest in some no-dose, or I could use that no-dream spell I found as a witchling." After I'd seen *Nightmare on Elm Street* for the first time when I was about seven, I went in search of a spell to keep me from dreaming, just in case. As part of the supernatural world, I was well aware that worse things than the fictional character of Freddy Kruger existed, and some of them could claw their way into dreams.

"Neither would do you any good. I would still bring you here."

"Of course you would. So what is it now?"

Thump-thump, thump-thump, thump-thump ...

I opened my eyes, unable to resist looking any longer. Just like before, Makoto's spirit heart rested in Kiernan's leather-clad hand. "Must you taunt me with that?"

I sensed Kiernan's smile, even though his face was cloaked within his hood. "It's to show you that no harm has befallen it ... yet."

"Yeah, okay." We both knew it was more than that. Maybe he wanted to show me Makoto's heart was still beating, but he also wanted to taunt me. It served both purposes. "Again, what do you want?"

"I want that charm."

"What? The fae charm?"

"Yes."

"I don't have it."

"So get it."

"I—"

Thump-thump, thump-thump, thump-thump ...

I nodded instead of protesting. I really was at Kiernan's mercy until he gave Makoto back his spirit heart. *And then I'll make you pay.* "Fine. Now stop bothering me."

Thump-thump, thump-thump, thump-thump ...

"Good little *cailleach*."

The aroma of fresh food, some kind of stew, zinged up my nose, causing my mouth to pool with saliva. My eyes popped open as a tray with a brightly colored spread was placed in front of me.

I groaned and pinched the bridge of my nose. "I can't eat any of this."

"Why not?" Prince Anyon demanded. "I, the crown prince of the Light Court, soon to be King, procured you your meal myself."

"Exactly. It's fae food. Everyone knows not to eat fae food."

"Rems." Makoto perched beside me, one side of his mouth curling up to form a smirk. "Those are just stories. Fae food may be different, but I can assure you it's harmless." To demonstrate, he popped a round pink wafer-looking thing into his mouth, chewing demonstratively. "It's not bad."

"Yeah, tell that to Alice."

"Alice was a stupid *cailleach*. Pretty, but stupid," Prince Anyon said. "Eating fae food is safe, unless you find it lying around. Everyone knows the lesser fae are prone to pranks. Alice got what she deserved for traipsing around unescorted on fae land. What had she been up to? Surely nothing good."

I snorted. "The lesser fae? All fae seem to find torturing other beings a source of amusement. And Alice was a child, just a little witchling. She fell into a fae portal. Not her fault. She probably didn't even realize where she was until it was too late."

I picked up one of the wafers Makoto had eaten and tentatively placed it on my tongue. I closed my eyes, chewing slowly, the flavor not something I could quite place, but it was good. Sort of. I forced myself to swallow.

"As I recall, one of your ancestors gave her an especially hard time to boot." In the end, Alice had become a cautionary tale for all witches, and the true story, albeit altered drastically, had somehow been turned into a human book.

I sampled the stew next, moaning with pleasure as the succulent dish warmed my insides. "Okay, fine, this is good even though I don't know what it is." I raised my hand before Prince Anyon or Makoto could say anything. "And don't tell me. I can't afford to puke up my only source of nutrients."

Makoto picked at the food on my tray, making sure I got my fill of everything before he fed himself. I met his gaze as I continued to eat my meal, considering everything. Things kept getting more and more complicated. I needed to come up with a solid plan on how to proceed with our current predicaments. We needed to get the fae charm from Crel for Kiernan, as well as find Kiernan's body. Then I was going to have to deal with my warlock father, and a possible war, which I still thought Prince Anyon was using to manipulate me … even still, one never knows. Oh, and how could I forget about the favors I owed the smoke demon? I was pretty sure I was leaving a few things out, but I could only concentrate on so many impending catastrophes at once.

Step one, getting Makoto's heart back. I narrowed my eyes at Prince Anyon, speaking around a mouthful of blue crunchy vegetables. At least I think they were vegetables. "Okay, I'll help you get the charm back from Crel."

"What?" Makoto attempted to school his shock. "I mean, good choice, Rems. But …" His gaze darkened, the indigo intermingling with first black, and then gold. He was worried and emotional. Completely unbalanced. Which was why I had to do what Kiernan demanded. I had to fix Makoto. No matter what else happened, nothing changed that from being my top priority.

I took a swig of some kind of sour juice, my face puckering slightly, before pausing to nibble on my lip. There was a very real possibility that Kiernan didn't intend to ever give Makoto back his heart. I'd already considered that possibility, and decided that so far, what Kiernan wanted in exchange was worth the risk. *But what if he eventually asks for something I can't deliver? Or what if he asks for more and more things until time runs out for my kitsune?*

I shook my head in an attempt to dislodge my dark thoughts. If I was to have any sense of hope about getting Makoto's heart back, I had to remain positive, no matter how naïve it made me feel.

I pushed the tray away, and swung my legs over the edge of the bed, eager to put some distance between me and the disgusting piece of furniture. It gave me the heebie-jeebies to think about what kind of bodily fluids I was probably contaminated with from Prince Anyon's bed. *I need a shower. A scalding shower and a wire brush to remove my top layer of skin. Ew.*

Makoto grabbed my elbow, steadying me, even though I didn't really need it. His breath was hot against the side of my face as he whispered, "Rems, what changed your mind about the charm?"

Does he know about Kiernan? I tightened the seal in my mind, making sure Makoto couldn't get in. I needed to tell him, but we also needed time to discuss it. I refused to just drop information on him without an explanation. "I just did. You were right. That kind of object of power can't fall into the wrong hands." Makoto snorted, but let the subject drop. I could sense that he wasn't buying what I was selling, especially because I wasn't letting him into my mind.

"I'll help you get the charm back, Prince Anyon. But I have a few conditions to go over first."

The prince nodded, his expression subdued. "I have a few of my own as well. For instance, you may not injure Crel in any way."

I threw my hands up in the air. "I can't make the promise."

Prince Anyon's face screwed up in thought. "Okay, then, you can't injure him permanently. Anything you do must be healable."

"Agreed. And here's the part where you tell me what his weaknesses are and how I'm going to be able to get close to him."

"He doesn't have any, except me."

I circled my temples with my forefingers. "Aw, come on. You have to work with me on this. There has to be something."

"Well, there is one thing ..."

R.

MY LIFE WAS the punchline to some epic joke. That was the only explanation for me walking around the Novem manor while waving a Nestle's Alpine White with Almonds chocolate bar in the air and hoping to draw the attention of an ancient dragon with it. Apparently Crel had a soft spot for the no longer manufactured bars, and Prince Anyon had the power to pull them through time. *I mean, really? Luring a dragon with chocolate? Gold, maybe … but chocolate?*

"Crel! Oh, Crel! I have something for you if you come out and talk to me!" I crinkled the wrapper demonstratively. "But you better hurry up because I'm getting hungry."

"Did he really think that would work?" a deep voice rumbled. "That I would trade his precious charm for a candy bar?"

I whirled, backing up a few paces as Crel emerged from the front door of the manor. "Well, you know Prince Anyon, he doesn't always think things through." My voice remained steady despite my nerves. Dealing with a crazy red dragon was not on my bucket list.

"Yes, *I* know Anyon, but how exactly do *you* know him?" There was no mistaking the accusation and jealousy in his tone.

"I'm just going to go ahead and lay it out there … I have never had any kind of sexual relations with Prince Anyon, nor do I want to."

Crel moved out into the open, the moonlight giving me my first good look at him. He was tall, at least six foot five or six foot six, his body holding the kind of muscles that were unusual for someone of his height. I knew he had red hair because of his dragon faction, but in the dim lighting, it appeared brown. It was cropped short, defining his high cheekbones and chiseled features. He wore faded jeans, a tight black T-shirt, and motorcycle boots. My gaze roamed up and down his body with appreciation. *Yeah, I see the appeal.* If anyone was going to get Prince Anyon to catch monogamy, Crel definitely had a higher-than-average shot.

Crel's eyes sparked and began to glow green, casting eerie shadows on his face. "Then why was he alone with you and the kitsune, if not to hide his relations with the two of you from me?"

I raised my hands in the air. "Look, buddy, I don't do fae, and Makoto is my familiar. Prince Anyon wanted to tell us about his mother in private."

Crel crossed his arms over his chest, his muscles bunching. "It's possible," he conceded. "But that doesn't change his other transgressions."

"Hey, I'm on your side. If you want to fry up his royal pain-in-the-ass, I'm not going to stop you. I'm just here for the charm."

"Why do you want it?"

"Does it matter as long as he doesn't get it back?"

Crel tilted his head, studying me. "You're powerful. It took me some time to escape your circle, and I'm still not sure how you managed to pull me into it. I don't think I'd be okay with handing something like the charm over to someone like you. What if you plan to do something nefarious with it?"

Nefarious, really? I waved the Nestle bar in the air, and his eyes tracked it. "Look, I need it. I can't tell you why, or for who for that matter, but someone is blackmailing me. And he wants that charm."

"What is he blackmailing you with?"

I sucked on my teeth, debating how much to tell Crel. I decided to go for broke. "He stole Makoto's spirit heart. Makoto isn't just my familiar—" My voice cracked. "Makoto is—I love him, and her—I love my kitsune, and I have to get that heart back before—"

"He turns to a dark kitsune. I'm familiar with what happens."

"Then you know why I need that charm. I came here, pretending that I was going to talk to you for Prince Anyon, but I'm not. I'm hoping you'll just give me the charm." I was met with silence. "Please."

"Does Anyon believe that I want to kill him?"

"Believe? Don't you?"

Crel ran his hand over his hair, sighing heavily. "Yes. No. Maybe."

I smirked. "I'll take that as a no. So about that charm . . ."

"I want him. I want to claim him. If I plan to be with him for all eternity, then I can't let the charm out of my sight. He's going to need it to rule the Light Court."

My heart sank into my stomach. "Please. I need it."

"Maybe I can convince Anyon to let you borrow it."

"Borrow it?" My mouth dropped open, hanging there, ready to catch any nearby flies.

"There has to be a way for all of us to get what we want."

I laughed, the sound devoid of humor. "How old are you? And you still think life is fair? That everyone will be able to get what they want?"

"We all have to believe in something."

"Yeah, well, I believe in me." I dropped the chocolate bar and raised my hands. "Makoto, now!"

A stream of fox-fire raced towards Crel, illuminating the night. It hit into his side, and he staggered. Just like we'd hoped, he'd been completely unprepared for the attack. It was the only way to harm a dragon with fire, by taking him completely by surprise so he couldn't raise his defenses. A moment later, I shot my own flame at Crel, weakening him even further.

"Stop! Please, stop!" Crel rasped.

"We won't kill you. At least I don't want to. Just give us the charm."

"I can't. I can't do that to Anyon."

"Yeah, well, you're not really doing anything."

Makoto and I continued to pummel Crel with our fire magic until he curled into a fetal position, the scent of burning hair and flesh filling the air. I gagged a bit, the odor pungent. "That's enough!" I yelled, withdrawing my magic. But Makoto didn't stop, didn't waver, didn't even give pause. Panic welled within me. Maybe it was too much for him. Maybe his temper was getting the best of him.

"That's enough!" I repeated, but with more force. *I'll do it, Makoto. I'll do it and then you'll hate me for it. I'll force my will on you through our familiar bond.*

The fox-fire stopped abruptly, and I sprinted to Crel, crouching over his now prone form. His clothes had burned away, and the charm I so desperately needed, hung around his neck, glittering ominously. I stared at it for a moment, wondering how something so simple-looking could be so powerful. It was silver toned, just a small round disk, utterly smooth with no markings, hanging from a thin chain. If I didn't know what it was, I would never have given it a second glance. It didn't even register on my magical radar. But there was no doubt it worked, just being near it made both Makoto and me stronger.

"I'm sorry," I whispered, snatching it from him, the chain snapping instantly. Although I wasn't sure if I was sorry for what I'd done or for possibly making an enemy out of him—and Prince Anyon. *I really don't need any more of those.*

Crel groaned, his eyes fluttering but not opening. He was in bad shape, his flesh blackened in spots, bone showing in others. But I knew dragons healed quickly, and if Prince Anyon aided him, which I knew he would, Crel would be as good as new. And isn't that what I'd promised Prince Anyon—to get the charm, which I did, and to not harm Crel past the point of healing? I'd found a loophole in our bargain, the prince being too eager for my help, him overlooking things he normally wouldn't have. Still, something akin to remorse knotted my stomach. I leaned in, whispering in Crel's ear, "He loves you. Prince Anyon loves you. I'm sure of it. He's fae—and scared. Don't give up on him."

I stood and draped the charm around my neck, the tiny hairs on my body rising when I fused the chain together, the hum of the charm's magic foreign, but not completely unwelcome. *I guess it has to be worn to feel its power.*

Makoto finally decided to join me, but in fox form. His multi-layered voice did little to hide his agitation. "When were you going to tell me about Kiernan? About him wanting the charm?'

"I just did."

Makoto's tails twitched back and forth. "I thought we weren't going to keep secrets from each other anymore."

"It wasn't a secret. I simply couldn't talk about my plans to double cross Prince Anyon ... in front of Prince Anyon."

I hurried towards the woods, scanning for Eve. Makoto dashed in front of me, its tails fluttering in the air. "You couldn't have thought it at me?"

"No," I snapped. "I needed to explain."

"I'm waiting," Makoto growled.

"We don't have time for this now. It's only a matter of time before Prince Anyon comes creeping around to try and find out what's going on and when he discovers Crel he's not going to be a happy fae prince." *Understatement of the year.*

"Mama! I found the portal!" Eve exclaimed, dashing towards me, her arms waving above her head with excitement. "This way!"

"Cailleach!" Prince Anyon's voice echoed through the woods, thunder cracking above us. "You'll pay for this! I swear it!"

"Shit!" Adrenaline surged through me. "Once we cross over into Alternum, we need to do a masking spell."

"But if we get separated—"

"We won't. And if we don't do the spell, we have zero chance of Prince Anyon not tracking us down in his home realm."

"Mama! Hurry!"

Portals to Alternum were undetectable by the naked eye, which was why stories of humans ending up in strange lands were so persistent. They were based in reality. That's why one moment I was running through the forest, and the next, I was gripped by the abrupt sensation of falling.

Chapter 9

I was on my back, staring up at the purple sky. "Makoto? Eve?" I croaked. "Everyone okay?"

Eve's lopsided roundish face appeared above mine. "That was fun!"

I sat up, rubbing my back. "Yeah, super fun."

I crawled on my hands and knees over to Makoto, who was lying a few feet away. "Makoto?"

Its fox head lifted, indigo eyes narrowed. "I hate those portals. They just spit you right out." A flash of purple revealed Makoto in her original female form, her kimono askew.

On wobbly legs I stood, offering my hand. A jolt of electricity passed between us when Makoto touched me, and she drew back sharply. "Damn fae portals. It's like super static cling."

I couldn't help but laugh at Makoto's scrunched up face. She was adorable when she got mad … well, when she was mad at something other than me. "It'll discharge as soon as we do the masking spell. You ready?"

She nodded, and I raised my hands hip level, palms up. "Those who seek us, pass by without notice, for we are one with our surroundings." I frowned, bitterness moving through my mouth and over my tongue. Usually, the taste would signal a spell gone wrong, but in Alternum it merely meant things worked slightly different. I sent up a silent prayer to the gods that I wasn't still recovering from Somniare, and I could pull off the masking spell with ease.

Magic shot out from me, zinging around erratically, before rising up above us, and exploding like fireworks. Sparks of color rained down on us, completing the spell. I grinned, fingering the charm around my neck. "You know, I've had this thing for all of five minutes, and I already know I'm going to miss it."

"Mama! This way!" Eve darted off, only the top of her head visible in the tall grass. I focused on her blue and purple pigtails, trailing along after her.

Makoto drew up next to me. "Anything else you want to fill me in on?"

My mind immediately went to the three favors I owed the shadow demon, but I couldn't bring myself to broach the subject. "Nope. Kiernan pulling me into Somniare when I was asleep to demand the charm is about it."

Makoto sighed. "I don't like this, Rems, any of it."

I brushed my fingers over the familiar brand on her wrist. "I'm sorry about threatening to use this. I didn't know what else to do."

She slipped her hand into mine, squeezing. "I get it. I was out of control."

"It scares me to see you that way. I've always been the hot-headed one."

She swallowed audibly. "It scares me, too."

Snarls erupted behind us, and Makoto and I turned in unison. "*Cu Siths!*" An entire pack of them were charging us, razor sharp teeth glinting in the sun. Makoto dropped my hand, both of us turning to run.

"Where the hell did they come from?" I squeaked.

"The Alpha is wearing a gold collar."

Cu Siths were pack animals, much like wolves. In order to compel an entire pack, all that was needed was complete control over the Alpha, which obviously someone had. *But how did they find us with my masking spell?* They either had to have been lying in wait, knowing exactly what to expect so they could see past my magical barrier, or something was wonky with my magic. *Shit. Either answer is not good.*

I hadn't noticed the little detail about the gold collar, but that made what was happening even worse. If a random pack of *Cu Siths* had just happened upon us because of my magic not working quite right, they were dangerous, but they'd be easy enough to lose. If they were sent after us, they wouldn't stop until they tore us limb from limb. The problem was: I didn't want to kill the *Cu Siths* if it was at all possible. They were wild animals, and it wasn't their fault they were being used as pawns. Truthfully, it pained me more to think about harming a *Cu Sith*, than it did most humanoid creatures.

Anger and indignation for the *Cu Siths* boiled within me. *Who the hell is controlling them?* I quickly ruled out my father, because he wanted me alive so he could steal Callie's necromancy magic. It also wasn't Prince Anyon since he'd been present when we'd discovered the first *Cu Sith* with a golden collar. It definitely wasn't Kiernan. *So who does that leave?*

Think, think, think ... we can't just outrun them. We need to do something.

I growled under my breath, steeling myself for the inevitable. I wouldn't hesitate to kill if I had to. It didn't matter if I wished for an alternative. With the control of a third unknown party ... it was us or them.

I lobbed a sphere of magic over my shoulder, hoping it hit one of the *Cu Siths*. When no whimpers or yelps met my ears, I lobbed a few more.

"I can try fox-fire."

I glanced over as Makoto drew her flame around her, charging it. "No! We don't know how it'll react in Alternum. Don't risk it."

"Well then, what do you suggest? Tarik? He might not be able to get through to this realm easily. You know the fae set up wards."

"Hold on, let me think."

"Think fast! They're gaining on us!"

Had I missed the *Cu Sith* on purpose? *Yes.* I was still holding out hope that I wouldn't have to do what I was about to do. My spheres of magic were meant to scare, not maim. That was about to change. And I hated that fact.

I pivoted on my heels, my dark hair flying into my face, obscuring my view. "Tarik! I need you!" The buzz of Tarik's energy warmed my hand, but he didn't take form. He was trying to get to me, but as Makoto had predicted, was having difficulty because of where we were. "Please, Tarik! Try harder!"

The charm and its chain heated, burning against my clavicle and sternum. Suddenly Tarik took corporeal form, blazing a bright purple. But just like the last time he'd come to me, no magical armor accompanied him. *I need to figure out why. But later, no time now.*

Despite my reluctance to battle the *Cu Siths*, the moment Tarik was in my hand, all hesitance vanished as I let his mood guide me. He was always ready for a fight, and since the *Cu Siths* were threatening us, Tarik had no remorse when it came to killing them.

I ran headlong for the Alpha, holding Tarik to the side, and low. When the Alpha leapt for me, teeth curled back to expose its razor sharp fangs, I stepped to the side, slashing Tarik's blade across its flank. Immediately the rest of the pack, seven or eight of them, adjusted their trajectory to take me down, their Alpha lying in a heap in the grass.

I spun, cutting through the first few *Cu Siths* as I whirled back around. I jumped over one that had fallen at my feet, and jabbed Tarik into another's back, kicking yet another in the face to buy me some time. I slashed at two more before stabbing at the one I'd kicked in the face. I glanced around, noting that I'd injured all in the pack, some worse than others. Uncertainty warred … not just within me, but in Tarik as well. Technically we'd taken out the threat, but would it be better to actually kill them all, put them out of their misery? Or walk away, hoping for their possible recovery?

"Tarik," Makoto called. "Come to me, now."

The katana blinked out of my hand, appearing a moment later in Makoto's. Because of our tight bond, sometimes I forgot that Tarik technically belonged to my kitsune, since I used him so often.

Makoto glided forward, her face a mask of calm. She moved quickly and efficiently through the ranks of the fallen *Cu Sith* pack, dispensing each one stoically. When she was finished, she snatched the golden collar from the dead Alpha, and met my gaze, hers cold and indifferent.

"It had to be done?" I hadn't meant it to be, but it'd come out a question. I wasn't sure if the decision to kill the pack was one that Makoto would have made prior to losing her spirit heart, although it might have been. Mercy is sometimes the only thing you can give a creature in such a situation. The thing was, I still wasn't sure if that was true in the current one.

"Yes, it did. As soon as they were healed, they would have come after us again."

"And who's to say that whoever sent these won't send more?"

She tucked the collar into her kimono, and wiped

Tarik off in the grass, an unnecessary move, but one that I'd done myself at times. "And whoever it is probably will send more, it would have just doubled the danger for us. Obviously your spell didn't work on them." She closed her eyes and spun in a circle, before facing me once more. "I don't detect any holes though. The magic feels sound. I'm not sure how they found us. Which is another reason we couldn't risk letting them live."

I nodded, knowing she was right, but hating having to be in the situation at all. "Yeah, okay. Let's get a move on."

"Mama?" Eve parted some grass, peering up at me from a few feet away.

"Go ahead, lead the way, we're right behind you."

There were too many unknown players in the game. Too many variables. I just wanted to do what Kiernan wanted and get Makoto's spirit heart back. I was tired of doubting my kitsune. I hated looking at her and wondering if her decisions were right or wrong. She'd always been the voice of reason—the wise one in our relationship. But now it was as if a part of her had become a stranger.

I glanced over at Makoto, who was shuffling along beside me, head hanging low. My heart squeezed. It had to be just as confusing for her. I grabbed her hand and pulled her into my side. "I'm here. You can lean on me."

And she did.

Her soft hair tickled my nose as she pressed her head against my shoulder, her flowery scent swirling around me. I slid my arm down, wrapping it around her waist, offering her physical support. Her breathing stuttered, becoming ragged. Dampness penetrated my shirt as silent tears dripped from her long lashes. I didn't say anything else, letting her sift through her emotions on her own, letting her know I was there for her if she wanted to talk. I just hoped, if and when the time came, she'd lean on me metaphorically as well.

Chapter 10

My thoughts wandered to my father as we made our way to find Kiernan's body. Normally Alternum was dazzling—beautiful because it was different than Mundi, and I'd never spent enough time there to have become accustomed to it on any level. But not even the vibrant colors of the vegetation, skies, and local inhabitants could draw my eye. Not when I was still trying to wrap my mind around the fact that my own father had murdered my sister, and then had mourned her with the rest of Domus Novem.

Why was he after the necromancy gift? My sister claimed it was to raise an army, but even if that part was true, why? My father had never seemed all that interested in status, or rising up in the social ranks of Domus Novem. If he was so concerned with domination of any kind, wouldn't he have shown some kind of prior signs?

Something to point at his maniacal tendencies? No one was that good of an actor. There had to be some underlying motivation that I didn't know about. Something had changed along the line.

But what? What is it?

Just like with any parent, sometimes it was hard to think of my father as anything but that … my father. I only knew what he wanted me to know, and even then, there was so much I'd been kept in the dark about. Not every witch was a part of a domos magicae—in fact, most weren't. My father hadn't grown up as a Novem and had only become one when he'd met and fallen in love with my mother. If he'd ever loved her to begin with. What if he had some secret agenda their entire relationship? What if he'd pretended to love my mother, and the rest of us were just a means to an end?

Or maybe none of his motivations mattered. Maybe I just wanted there to be more, like there turned out to be with my mother. But I'd seen what had happened between my father and Callie, and if he truly was responsible for the warlocks in Somniare, he'd tried to kill me, too. It didn't matter why he wanted the necromancy power. Any male who would kill his own children for any kind of power didn't deserve a chance for explanation. He deserved karma.

"Rems." Makoto bumped her shoulder against mine. "Stop thinking about him. It won't do you any good."

I nibbled on my thumbnail, meeting Makoto's indigo

gaze. "I can't seem to help myself. I just want to understand why."

She slapped the back of my hand. "Stop biting your nails."

"There's no one here to see besides you and Eve," I huffed. "Let it go, I'm stressed."

"If you make it a habit—"

Several fae royal guards appeared about ten feet from us. "Eve!" I hissed, motioning for her to come to me.

Scrambling to my side, she hugged my leg. "The spell should work, Mama. Don't worry."

"Quiet," Makoto whispered.

Makoto was obviously thinking the same thing I was. If my spell had worked perfectly, the fae wouldn't be anywhere close to us. I didn't believe in coincidences, so it wasn't one that the guards had shown up where we were. My spell was only partially working, which meant if we remained perfectly still, not drawing attention to ourselves, then there was a chance they'd move on to search for us elsewhere. Or at least I hoped. After all, the *Cu Siths* had tracked us with ease. I pushed a little extra magic into the cloaking spell, hoping it would flow to wherever the hole was. *Why the hell didn't I rework it before? Over confidence is going to be my downfall one day.*

My muscles tensed as I sucked in shallow breaths, my heart quadrupling in time. I didn't even dare turn my head as I tracked the guards' movements with only my eyes.

"They couldn't have gotten too far, they're moving on foot."

How did they know we were moving on foot? How did they know we hadn't procured some kind of flying incantation or even harnessed a fae beast with the power of flight? My spell was supposed to make us blend in, and that included everything that went along with hiding our trail, like footprints, broken branches, basically anything that natural born trackers, like the fae, could use to find us. It was difficult not to panic when I didn't know which part of my casting wasn't working. It could be any little piece, but if I knew, I could strengthen it, or at least be prepared. *Damnit, if I was in Mundi I would be able to tell with ease where the problem is.* Instead, I felt like I was walking a tightrope without a net.

One of the guards, his armor burnished a reddish gold by the setting sun, marched towards me, pausing a few steps away. His sapphire gaze moved over me, lingering in my direction for a moment, before he turned to rejoin his compadres, who were searching randomly around.

"I don't see any trace of them," one of the guards called from across the field.

"Me neither," another yelled.

"We need to find them. Prince Anyon demands it."

They all disappeared as suddenly as they had appeared.

As I set down Eve, I let out a long, loud breath, before expanding my chest fully. "That was too close for my liking. You need to check my spell again, Makoto. What part isn't right?"

"Your spell's fine. They were just guessing because of the *Cu Siths*, and Prince Anyon knows we're on foot."

"But how did he know we're still in Alternum? We could have just as easily jumped back after we lost him."

"The wards."

Of course, the wards would let him know that we hadn't exited, but not where we were. I'd forgotten. *Get your shit together, Remy.* "We better get a move on, because we might not be as lucky next time."

I lumbered after Eve, exhaustion beginning to take hold. When Makoto didn't move to follow, I stopped to study her. "You coming?"

Makoto tugged at a braid in her hair, her gaze vacant. Slowly a smile began to stretch her full lips, turning her expression gleeful. "I'm going to make sure they don't follow us first." She snapped her fingers rapidly, and with each time, a sphere of fox-fire exploded into existence, hovering near her.

"Makoto, what—"

Before I could finish my question, she rose up off the ground. "Lead me to them." The fox-fire shot across the field, faster than my eyes could follow, Makoto flying behind the spheres, nothing but a blur.

"Don't wait for me. I'll find you," her voice sounded in my head.

I didn't doubt she could, since my masking spell was less than perfect, even still … My heart dropped into my feet, as a lump formed in my throat. *This isn't like her.* Whatever it was that Makoto was planning was definitely because of her missing spirit heart, the imbalance it caused affecting her emotions more and more. *Please don't let her do something she'll regret.*

Kitsunes were known in some lore as being demon foxes, but it was the yako kitsune that had earned that reputation. They exemplified every negative characteristic of both the male and female energies. They behaved rashly, were vindictive, spiteful, jealous … pretty much everything one might think of that would be a negative or character flaw. And Makoto would become like that—if I didn't get her heart back before the shift in her was complete.

I'm wasting time standing here thinking about this. I need to keep going, with or without Makoto, to find Kiernan. It's the only way I can fix things.

But without Makoto by my side, the weight of everything sat heavier on my shoulders, the pressure of it stifling. *What if I fail?* I trudged forward, my footsteps laden down by a combination of morose thoughts, exhaustion, and hunger. I kept my eyes trained on Eve's blue and purple pigtails, numbly lumbering along after her, forcing myself forward when my body and mind were screaming for me to stop.

Just a five-minute break. Just five minutes.

As soon as I gave myself permission, I collapsed, crumpling in on myself. "Five minutes, Eve. Give me five minutes." I thought I heard her say something, her voice unsure as her tiny burlap hand moved over my face, but I was tugged into unconsciousness almost instantly.

"WAKE UP, *CAILLEACH.*"

My eyes fluttered but refused to obey. I groaned, just wanting to be left alone.

"You need to wake up. You're so close. I can feel it."

"Kiernan?" I peeled one eyelid open, struggling to focus.

"Yes, it's me." He leaned in, his ice blue eyes boring into mine from mere inches away. "You're close to my body. You need to wake up and keep going."

"I know I'm a witch, a magical being, but unlike in Somniare, I need sleep and food. There aren't any spells that can replace either without horrible side effects."

"What you ate before wasn't enough?" He sounded genuinely perplexed.

"No. Or well, it was at the time, but I need to eat several times a day." When I was met with silence, I decided to clarify. "Fae don't need to eat. They derive energy of all kinds from their surroundings. They eat because they're hedonists by nature and they enjoy it. But they don't eat for the same reasons as someone like me would."

"Can't you do what the fae do and get energy from your surroundings? You're going to attempt to tell me that you stole my magic from me, nearly sucked me dry, and you don't have the ability to do something so mundane? I don't believe that for a second."

I sighed, squeezing my eyes shut. "In theory I could do it. But I'm not from Alternum. If I could re-energize myself that way, I'd need to get the energy from Mundi, the realm I was born in."

"You are part fae, in a sense, because of my magic. Wake up and take what your body needs from the fae environment."

My eyes popped open, and I met his glacial gaze again. "I'm not fae at all." I pushed down a shudder of revulsion.

He grinned. "Oh, but you are. You're even more of an abomination than I am." He picked up a piece of my dark hair, and twirled it around his index finger, yanking. "You're a witch with dark fae magic running through your veins, and the power of necromancy. Oh," he yanked again, causing me to grimace, "let's not forget about the relationship you have with your familiar."

My lips curled back from my teeth, and I spoke through gritted teeth. "None of those things make me an abomination. And nothing in existence in any realm is more of an abomination than a goblin."

Kiernan's fingers curled into my hair tightly. "I'd watch what you say to me, little *cailleach*. I'm about to be unleashed in your world and you don't want me as an enemy."

I snorted. "What's one more at this point?" My heart sped up despite my cavalier words. Having Kiernan, the rightful goblin king, and someone who could track me to the ends of any realm for the rest of my life because he'd sampled my blood—yeah, having him as an enemy would definitely not be good.

Kiernan released me, my head falling back to hit the

ground. "Good, now that we understand who holds the power position … wake up and use the fae in you to restore your body's energy."

I bit the inside of my cheek, forcing myself to swallow the rest of the snide comments I had waiting on my tongue. "Show me Makoto's heart first." Despite my disorientation, and inability to distinguish anything around me besides Kiernan, I hadn't missed the little detail that it was the first time Makoto's heart wasn't being lorded over me.

Thump … thump … thump-thump … thump …

Terror constricted my breathing. "It's dying."

"Yes. So you better hurry."

The sluggish rhythm of Makoto's heart echoed through my mind, ricocheting from one side to the other, winding its way around my chest, squeezing.

"Send me back. Now," I croaked.

Kiernan tucked the heart away and reached over to pat me on the head. "Good little *cailleach*."

For the thousandth time, I swore to myself that I would make him pay one way or another.

Chapter 11

The thing about magic, real magic, not the kind that humans are sometimes able to dabble in, but the kind that flows through your veins and is pumped through your blood, is that words and spells aren't necessary. Candles, talismans, symbols … they're all used to keep a powerful being in check. If I had called my mother's spirit without having a circle to focus my energy, I would have ended up yanking every spirit within earshot to me. As it was, I'd somehow pulled Crel into the fold. Or, if I hadn't used the blood magic symbols when I'd called the shadow demon to me, I might have released a legion of demons. Sometimes potions or powders are used, but not for truly strong magic. And rare charms existed, like the fae object around my neck, which were imbibed with power of their own.

I'd always struggled with controlling my powers. I needed focus objects to keep me from going too big with my magic. I'd spent most of my adolescence trying not to blow things up or inadvertently kill someone. If I had ascended to my full powers and the position of Grand Witch, I would have been tempered, balanced, and retrained by the rest of domos magicae—but that would never happen, and with each day I was growing stronger —more dangerous. Makoto, as my familiar, was also a focus. With my kitsune near, it grounded me in a way that nothing else did. I knew that one day, now that I wouldn't be a Grand Witch of anything, I'd have to find a permanent solution to my problem, if there even was one. A witch as powerful as me wasn't meant to go unchecked, and I was pretty sure it'd never happened before—at least not without catastrophic results.

As my consciousness returned to my body, trepidation knotted my gut. How the hell was I supposed to draw Alternum energy into myself without Makoto, and without having ever done it before? The process, even if I was in Mundi, had never been performed by me. Even though, in theory, because I had the ability to do it, I should be able to just ... do it.

I sat up, attempting to rub the fatigue from my eyes, everything around me a blur. *You can do this. Make it quick. You don't have time to fret over your skills when Makoto's spirit heart is dying.*

"Come to me!" I commanded, my head thrown back. In my mind's eye, I pictured tiny particles of energy, just a little from everything around me, even the dirt itself, racing towards me, and being absorbed into my body. A zing of energy jolted my system, which I took as a good sign. "Come to me!" I said louder, wiggling my fingers as if reaching for the imagined particles.

Electricity shocked my system, and my body rose off the ground, arching sharply. I blinked rapidly, surprise rounding my eyes as I stared above me. Just like I'd imagined, tiny particles, resembling golden glitter, filled the air around me. I flailed, panicking, and dropped to the ground. The spell ended, leaving me to take in the utter devastation surrounding me. Plants were wilted and browned, animals and birds lay on the ground, still or gasping for breath—everything within a seemingly cylindrical shape were dead or dying, like I had ripped their life-force right out of them.

I sat there in the midst of the decay, frozen by guilt and remorse. Maybe I didn't mind the plants so much—after all, it was to give me nourishment when I had none—but the rest hollowed out my chest. *I'm sorry. I didn't mean to kill anything.*

I crawled forward on my hands and knees, brittle grass snapping under me, the stale aroma of the surrounding plants reminding me of fall, which was almost pleasant. I peered down at a dead bird. It was small, its head turned to the side, its eyes closed. It could have been mistaken for sleeping, the scene emanating peace, if I didn't know better. But I did. Its colorful yellow feathers were already dull, death having touched it too soon. *Was it happily flying along, singing a cheerful melody when I struck it down? What if it had a nest of baby birds it needed to get to?*

I pressed a hand to my mouth, muffling a sob. "I'm sorry," I whispered. "I'm so sorry."

Unable to help myself for some inexplicable reason, I gently cupped the bird, lifting it off the ground. "I wish you could live. I wish I could save at least you."

The bird came to life in my hands. Utterly terrified, it pecked at my index finger, its tiny wings frantically flapping, before shooting off into the air, disappearing into the distance a moment better. I fell back onto my haunches, stunned. *I brought it back to life.* I wasn't exactly sure what that meant either. I didn't know the rules of necromancy. Would the bird's body decompose and rot, its spirit trapped in a lifeless vessel? Or did I repair its body when I'd brought it back to life? I shook my head to dislodge the sudden image of a zombie bird attacking me. *Ick.*

"Mama?" Eve leaned into my side, reminding me of her presence. "Are you ready to find Kiernan now?"

I turned to study my living voodoo doll, wondering if I'd somehow given her life in Somniare by using my then unknown necromancy gift. *I'd leaked magic to give her life, but what kind?* But even if I'd unwittingly used necromancy magic, how had Kiernan done it the second time? Or maybe the current version of my doll wasn't alive in the same way she'd been in Somniare, maybe she was merely a facsimile created to manipulate my emotions.

Pushing all my current questions aside, I pulled myself to my feet and motioned to Eve. "Go ahead, lead the way."

She raced off, her stubby legs moving faster than I'd ever seen them go. I had to sprint to keep up with her. Luckily, I was full of energy, and my thoughts were no longer consumed with food, water, or sleep.

"It's not too far from here, Mama."

Excitement caused my belly to do a flip-flop. *Is it almost really over?*

A few thousand heartbeats later, farther than I thought it would be, Eve halted abruptly, jumping up and down, her sewn-on smile ready to pop a stitch. "Mama, here! Here, here, here!"

"I don't see anything." We were standing in the middle of an open field, much like the many open fields we'd already passed through. "Where exactly is here?"

"Kiernan's body is buried here." She stomped her foot repeatedly on the ground. "Right below here."

"His body is buried? Great." As cliché as it sounded, I'd expected a dark and foreboding cave, or a special rock formation that I'd have to use magic to bust open, at the very least, a tree that opened up or … something simpler, and a bit more dramatic. "So I guess we dig?"

"Yes," Eve said. "Right here."

"Happen to know how far down we're going?"

She tilted her head as if she was listening to something. "No," she finally responded. "Just until we hit the box he's in."

"Riiiight," I drawled, frustration replacing the excitement I'd been feeling moments before. How the hell was I supposed to dig without a shovel? Could I just fling dirt with magic? It was definitely something I never thought about before.

"There's a ward on this area," Makoto's voice interrupted my thoughts. "You can't simply use magic to dig."

"Makoto!" I exclaimed, blindly rushing my kitsune. I was so happy to see ... him—he was back to his original male form—but he was covered in blood. I stopped short, dropping my eager arms that I longed to throw around him. "Wh-what happened? You're not hurt are you?" My chest constricted, magic at the ready to heal.

He laughed, his eyes glinting with arrogance. "None of this is my blood." He notched his chin up. "I took care of those fae guards just like I said I would."

I swallowed, my gaze traveling over my kitsune, taking in the amount of blood on him. There was so much of it ... spattered all over the front of his kimono, and even a few streaks marred his white hair. "What did you do to them?"

He leaned against a tree, crossing his arms and legs. "Killed them, of course."

"But fae are nearly impossible to kill. And they were royal guards. Harder than most."

"It wasn't a difficult task. Fae of any kind are not a match for a kitsune like me." Makoto pushed off the tree, swaggering over to me, his lips turning up into a smirk. "You don't appreciate me in so many ways." He drew a finger down the side of my neck, the nail scraping my skin. "But you're safe now. And I'm waiting for my thanks."

I lifted my gaze to his, the color of his eyes no longer indigo but a deeper shade, almost black. "Your thanks?"

His hand slipped into my hair, holding it tightly at the base of my neck. "Yes, your thanks."

Makoto had never asked for the words before, and I would have happily given them to him, but as he grazed his teeth along my jaw, his large frame pressing solidly against mine, I realized he wanted something else entirely.

All of my nerve endings came alive, sizzling under Makoto's touch. I melted into him, rational thought rushing from my body as he sealed his lips over mine. I groaned into his mouth, drinking down his succulent taste, while his hands freely roamed my body. I was giddy, drunk on Makoto's essence within moments.

Yet, when he ripped at my shirt, dread coiled within me, cooling my ardor like a bucket of ice over my head would, and I pushed at Makoto's chest. "Wait, just hold on a second." *This isn't right. He's not himself. I can feel it.* Even though I yearned for physical affection from Makoto, almost any way I could get it, he was acting too forceful somehow. The exact source of my distress was vague, winding anxiety through me, as I struggled to make sense of it.

It wasn't exactly *what* he was doing, but rather the attitude that was accompanying his actions. It wasn't passion that was driving his roughness with me, but entitlement. The Makoto standing in front of me now was a stranger, one that I didn't know if I could trust or not, and that changed everything.

"Like hell I'm gonna wait," he muttered. "I've waited long enough."

"Makoto." I shoved at him again when he yanked me back against his chest, his hips pivoting into mine.

"You belong to me, Rems. And it's damn time I take what's mine."

"You want our first time to be right here, right now?"

"I don't care where it is, Rems. As long as it happens now." He reached for me again, even as I moved away.

"It's not going to happen now, Makoto. You're—you're scaring me." Those words had worked before to bring him back from his dark place—the place of the yako kitsune. I just prayed they did again.

He sneered, the expression distressing under the circumstances. "Scaring you? Because I'm finally taking what you've been offering for so long? How many times have you pulled me into your bed over the last few years? How many times have you straddled me? Touched me? Silently begged for me to take you?" He shook his head. "I'm tired of being your good little kitsune."

I continued to back up, slapping at his hands as he pawed at me with no restraint. "You're not acting like yourself. The real you wouldn't shrug off my fears."

His eyes narrowed, flashing red, before bleeding into black. "The real me?" He thumped a hand against his chest. "This is the real me." He snatched my wrist, yanking me into him. "Every part of me has always wanted you—

so much it hurts." He wrapped his arms around me, his nails digging into my spine as he molded himself around me. His breath tickled my ear when he whispered, "I don't want to hurt anymore, Rems. I need you."

I trembled within his embrace, afraid for the both of us. Even though Makoto was acting like an ass, he was still my kitsune, still the one I loved, and had loved for as long as I could remember. He was hurting, that much was true. But from more than just being denied intimacy with me.

"I do want you, Makoto. I'll always want you. But not like this."

He kissed a heated trail down the side of my neck, scorching my flesh. I was positive there'd be physical marks left behind. "You'll change your mind. I'll make it good. I promise. It'll ease things for both of us." Goose bumps erupted along my skin, and a small moan escaped my parted lips.

"That's right, Rems, let me love you like I've wanted for so long."

I fisted my hands in his hair, torn between wanting to pull him tightly against me or yank him away, my desires warring. "Makoto ... please." The problem was, I wasn't even sure what I was asking for. Did I want him to keep going, or to stop? *Maybe both?*

"Makoto ... no. Stop. Our first time can't be here, like this." I wrenched his neck back, my gaze meeting his fathomless black depths. "We'll get you back your spirit heart, and everything will be okay."

He snarled, his canines elongating into fangs, his voice

143

guttural. "I don't care about that thing anymore. I just want you. The only thing I care about is you."

I knew with absolute certainty that there was no getting through to him, at least in that moment. There was only one thing I could do. *Please let him forgive me later.* "Makoto, I command you as my familiar to stop." I'd never used the magic before, but within the brand on Makoto's wrist was a binding magic, which allowed me to bend him to my will.

He rocked back from me, his eyes wild as he clawed at the inside of his wrist, the place where my brand was. "How could you?" His tone was filled with accusation and hurt. "How could you?" he repeated, dropping to the ground. He clutched his wrist to his chest, hunching over as he rocked back and forth. "I can't believe you would do that to me."

Even though Makoto had officially bonded with me as my familiar, he'd been more to me since day one. A playmate, a best friend, the one I loved. There had been an unspoken promise that despite outward appearances, we were equals, and I wouldn't use the bond to compel him. The mark on his wrist was meant to link us together in a way that couldn't be broken. The only bond stronger would be if Makoto took me as his mate.

I bit my lower lip, hating what I'd done, but knowing it'd been necessary in the long run. Makoto may claim to not care about his spirit heart, but that admission only ratcheted it up higher in importance to me. And I was so close. "I'm sorry," I rasped. "You have no idea how much."

I turned away from him, eyeing the ground that housed Kiernan's body. Eve had flopped in a heap, leaning on a small rock, attention absorbed in jabbing her pins in and then out of her stuffed limbs.

I'd never felt so alone in my entire life. Even in Somniare, when I hadn't remembered Makoto, and had given my kitsune the ridiculous name of Unagi, I still sensed the bond between us, I knew that now. My heart had remembered even when my mind hadn't. Now? Now, it was as if I'd lost Makoto on some level, and it gutted me, making it hard to breathe.

I dropped down onto my knees, digging into the dirt with my bare hands. *If I have to claw my way to Kiernan's body, inch by bloody inch, I will get Makoto's heart back. I refuse to truly lose my kitsune.*

Chapter 12

Minutes, hours, and maybe even days passed. All sense of time was lost to me as I dug. Sweat stung my eyes, and dripped down my face. My muscles shook with fatigue. I'd lost a few nails, the pain long since morphing to numbness … and still I persisted.

"Give it up. You'll never get to him," Makoto taunted. "You're an idiot if you think they didn't bury him hundreds of feet below ground. That's why they put him in Alternum, no power tools."

"Shut up." I swiped at my forehead with the back of my hand.

"You could compel me to help. Foxes are excellent diggers." His animosity rolled off of him in waves, threatening to drown me with the guilt of it.

"Keep it up, and I will."

Makoto's feet came into view a few moments later, the

hem of his kimono dark with dried blood. He could have cleaned himself a bit, but I knew he was using that to taunt me as well. He kicked a bit of dirt back into the hole I'd dug.

Yako kitsunes really are demon foxes.

"Stop."

"Why don't you compel me to?"

I stilled, fighting the very real urge to do just that. *So why don't you? He's already mad.* "Leave me alone," I grunted, scooping more dirt out of the way.

"I don't want to." He crouched, obviously set on having my full attention. "I'm bored."

"So help me or shut the hell up."

A flash of purple, and four white paws with razor-sharp nails flexed along the edge of the hole. "I'll help, but only because I don't want to be here forever, since you're determined to do this."

Relief washed over me. I hadn't wanted to admit it to myself, but after what had happened between us, and the attitude he'd been giving me, I was terrified that it was already too late for Makoto—that he had gone full yako. But him helping meant there was hope, even if it was microscopically small. Even the old Makoto would have had his feelings hurt because I'd compelled him. Kitsunes were wild spirits, not usually bound to anyone, except maybe a mate.

Makoto dug beside me, its front paws moving in a flurry of motion. Soon, we were another couple of feet down, and deep enough that I couldn't see the ground around us anymore. Time dragged on, both of us silent and intent on the task at hand, until finally …

"Is that?" I paused, pushing more dirt away. I'd come across several large stones before that had given false hope. I was almost afraid to let myself believe, and yet— "I think I hit it! I think this is it!"

Fresh energy surged through me, and a frenzy took over. With every little bit of the wooden box we uncovered the faster I dug. Finally, what felt like an eternity later, we'd fully uncovered it.

I reached for the latch, and Makoto grabbed my wrist. He'd changed back into his male original form without me noticing. "There could be magical booby traps."

"There probably are." There was a protection spell on the box, bare minimum, otherwise it wouldn't have remained so pristine all the years it'd been in the ground.

I laid my hands on the rough wood, smoothing my palms over the surface, scanning for magic. The hairs on my arms slowly lifted. "Protection, but that's it." I closed my eyes and tugged at the magic, searching for the binding threads. It was a simple spell, almost too simple, which made me think they'd done it for a reason. Probably to make sure the box was difficult to detect. Strong magic would have alerted many fae over the years to the presence of something beneath the soil, and someone would have dug long before we had.

When I found what I was looking for, I yanked the magic apart with my mind, instantly breaking the spell.

The box creaked, shifting as if it was sighing heavily. Makoto snapped the latch open, and I flung the lid back.

I sucked in a sharp breath. There in the middle of the box, as if he was merely sleeping, was a very young Kiernan, no more than eighteen or nineteen years old, if I had to guess. I hadn't considered, even though Kiernan had clued me in to it, that his soul alone had aged to maturity in Somniare.

"Do you suppose he's just going to wake up now?" *It can't be that simple.*

"Even though the protection spell has been collapsed, and his body could wake up, his spirit is in Somniare. He needs a way out."

I nibbled on my numb nail, spitting when I tasted dirt. "Will he need to kill someone, like I did?"

"No. You didn't have a body to return to. It was … murdered. Kiernan just needs to hitch a ride. His body isn't injured in any way."

"Right." I knew all of that. My body and mind were too fatigued to think straight. "I guess we need to both go in and get him so he can return your spirit heart to spirit you."

"No," Makoto snapped. "We can't go back there now. I'm afraid for you."

I lifted my head to take in his stark expression. "Why? We need to get your heart."

He lurched forward, wrapping his arms around me, his chin settling on the top of my head. "I know I acted like an ass. My emotions are harder to manage, but I can learn. I can learn to do anything for you. I don't need my spirit heart. Not really. I have a bad feeling about all of this—about your safety specifically."

I let his warmth comfort me as I pressed my nose into his neck. "I won't tell you that you're being paranoid. Nothing has truly been safe for us lately. Everything we've been doing has come with a hefty risk, but we still have to go. We can't let fear motivate us."

His grip tightened around me. "But we are letting fear motivate us. We're both afraid of what I'll become without my spirit heart. And ultimately because of that, we're both afraid of losing each other."

He was right. I'd let my fear of losing Makoto push me into a lot of things, especially lately. But some things couldn't be avoided. "We have to at least try to get your heart back."

"No. Please, Rems. I swear, I'll be fine without it. I'll just have to work at—"

I squeezed my eyes shut and willed us into Somniare.

$\mathcal{R}$

THUMP ... *thump ... thump ...*

Kiernan stood in front of us, waiting. Resting on his leather-clad hand was Makoto's spirit heart, beating slower than the last time I'd seen it. I reached for it on instinct, and he moved back to hold it just outside of my reach.

"Give it to me," I snarled. "It could die at any moment."

"Ah-ah-ah. Not just yet, *cailleach*."

"We found your body, and I got the stupid fae charm for you." I rubbed my thumb over the smooth round disk hanging around my neck, already lamenting the loss of its power. "I fulfilled my part of the bargain. Now give back Makoto's heart."

Kiernan extended his free hand. "Give me the charm, and then you can have the heart."

I slid the chain over my head, wincing when a few of my hairs went with it. "Here," I said, offering it to him. "Just take it."

"Bring it to me."

I glanced at Makoto, who was standing silently beside me, his gaze riveted to his heart. "Yeah, okay." I took one tentative step after another, closing the gap between Kiernan and me with aching slowness. I stopped when I was close enough where I could touch him, lifting my gaze to stare into his icy eyes.

"Put it on me," he commanded, his lips turning up into a sneer.

I ground my teeth together, imagining the many ways I wanted to hurt him. I stepped to his side and dropped the chain over his head, careful to touch him as little as possible.

"Ah, yes. I can feel it now." He rotated his head and rolled his shoulders, a pleased smile spreading across his face.

"Give me the heart." This was it. This was the moment

of truth. Would Kiernan actually give us back the heart, or would he double-cross us after everything?

"Of course." He flipped his hand over, the heart dropping towards the ground.

An involuntary cry escaped from me, as I dove to catch the heart. It passed just beyond my fingertips, landing in the dirt. I scrambled forward, as Kiernan stepped over me.

"Good luck getting that back into him."

"What? No." I hadn't even considered that part. "I … you need to put it back." I carefully picked up the heart, the feel of it in my hands strange. "Put it back!"

Kiernan turned to regard me. "That wasn't part of our bargain."

"You took it out—put it back. It was a given. It was a given." Tears, full of hate, streamed down my face, scalding my cheeks. Kiernan had never given me a chance to negotiate the terms of our agreement, since it was more blackmail on his part. I'd been so focused on the prize I hadn't considered the one gaping loophole. Or I hadn't wanted to see it. The latter was more likely.

"You have to put it back. Please." For Makoto, I would do anything, including beg a goblin I hated with every fiber of my being "Please. Please, you have to put it back. Please."

Makoto had come to stand by me, his movements gone unseen up until that point. He placed a hand on my shoulder. "We'll figure it out, Rems, we always do."

"No. He has to put it back." I crawled forward on my knees, Makoto's heart cradled within my hands.

Thump ... thump ... thump ...

"Please, it's dying. You have to put it back."

Kiernan leaned into me, grabbed a fistful of hair, and yanked my head to the side. "You sucked my magic dry in an attempt to kill me. If I'd been almost any other being, I would be dead."

"To save Makoto. I'd do anything for my kitsune. Anything. And I'll do anything now. Anything."

"Which is the only reason I haven't killed the both of you in retaliation." He wrenched my head further to the side, pain shooting down my neck. "But I couldn't let you go unpunished."

"Then punish me. Please. Punish me, not Makoto."

"By punishing your little kitsune, I am punishing you."

He released me, and I fell to the side, Makoto swooping me up in his arms before I could hit the ground fully. "You haven't won, Kiernan. You seek to punish her?" Makoto vibrated with anger. "I'll rain hell down on you." Fox-fire erupted around us, coloring everything a blue-ish purple.

"Your new fox-fire is impressive, but still no match for me, little kitsune." He snapped his fingers, disappearing from Somniare, using the path we'd taken in to finally get out of the dreamscape.

"Nooo!" I wailed. "Nooo!"

I'd failed Makoto. I was the cause of what was happening and I knew of no way to fix it.

"Shhh ... Rems. It'll be okay."

He was comforting me, when he was the one

suffering? No. I couldn't let that happen. *I can't afford to have an emotional breakdown right now. There has to be a way for me to put it back. There has to be a way. Time hasn't run out yet. As long as his heart beats, there's still time.*

I stared down at the tiny precious organ cupped within my hands. "If I can bring back a bird from the dead, why can't I do the same for a heart?" I lifted my gaze to meet Makoto's. "I could do it, right? If your heart dies before we can put it back in you … I can bring it back to life?"

"Maybe, if we remained here. But we can't take my spirit heart into the real world. It needs to be replaced in me here, while we're in Somniare, since that's where it was removed."

"Then we'll just stay here until we can figure it out. I know! I'll call the demon! He can do it." That was the answer. What was one more favor at this point? *I'll do anything for you, Makoto. Anything. Even sell my damn soul.*

"Rems." Makoto tucked my hair behind my ears and kissed my forehead. "No. I won't let you owe anything else for me. That just leaves the option of staying here until we figure out something else. And what about our bodies? We can't just leave them lying in Alternum unattended. This isn't like when we were here before. We can't stay here without risking something much worse than my spirit heart."

I shook my head, unwilling to accept it. "No. We'll figure it out. I'm going to fix you. I will."

"No. I've already accepted this. It's time you do, too."

He dropped me onto my ass, snatching his heart from my grasp.

"What are you doing?" I scrambled to my feet. "Makoto, stop!" The rest happened in slow motion, my body seemingly stuck in molasses as I lurched towards Makoto.

His fist closed around the heart, squeezing tightly. When his hand opened again, the heart was still and silent, dead. He upturned his hand, and for the second time that day, it tumbled into the dirt, only this time I didn't pick it up.

"It's done. Over," Makoto said, his head held high, and his gaze studiously not on the dead lump of flesh at his feet.

My lower lip trembled as I fought the urge to hit him. *Why? Why did you do that?* But I knew the answer. He'd done it for me. Just like I'd do anything for my kitsune— my kitsune would do anything for me, yako or not. *Maybe there's hope for us yet, despite the loss of his spirit heart.*

"Come on, Rems. Let's get back to our bodies."

I nodded once, taking his hand. The same one covered in his own heart's blood.

Closing my eyes, I willed us out of Somniare. Back to the real world, where the nightmares would be just as horrifying.

Chapter 13

My hands were yanked behind my back, my face pushed into the ground, and I choked on the scent of dirt and grass as weight was applied to my back. My voice was muffled, grit abrading my lips as I croaked out, "Makoto." I squirmed, managing to get one eye open, my view completely obscured by green.

"Rems, I'm here."

Someone screamed, the scent of burning flesh wafting up my nose. "Makoto!" I wriggled, the pressure on my back not letting up. "Makoto!" I couldn't see what was happening, had no clue what was going on, and something was binding my magic. *Is it Kiernan, is he doing this?*

"Get off of her!" Makoto snarled, more screams filling the air around me.

Not Kiernan. There's more than one person here, probably fae. I took an educated guess since I couldn't use my magic to sense anything. "Prince Anyon?" The question was directed at Makoto, but the subject in question answered himself.

"Yes, little dear little Remy. It's me. Did you think you'd escape my wrath so easily?"

"You don't understand. I had to. Plus, I didn't break our bargain ... exactly." I kicked my legs up, finding it did no good since I couldn't connect with anything.

A burst of flame surrounded me, but nothing happened. I wriggled more, only getting more dirt and grass in my nose and mouth. "Just let me explain."

"Let her up, Anyon. You won't win any points with me by hurting her or the kitsune." *Crel? Is Crel actually taking my side?* I had to be hearing things.

"No. She will pay for what she did to you." More pressure was applied to my back and I gasped for air.

"For me. Do it for me. Let her explain."

I was abruptly released, and I rolled over onto my back, the purple sky blurring as I sucked in a full lungful of air. "Just give ... me ... a ... second."

Crel crouched over me, a wry smile tipping up one side of his mouth. "Tell your kitsune to back off. He seems rather intent on killing everyone here, except you, of course." So why didn't Crel use his fire magic to protect everyone? Unless he was still weakened from what I'd done to him, which was probable.

I leaned up onto my elbows, searching for Makoto. Several fae royal guards lay in charred heaps, their blackened flesh almost unrecognizable at first glance. I wasn't sure if any of them were alive, or even if they were, if they were past the point of regeneration.

My heart stuttered in my chest when my gaze snagged on Makoto. He was—he was magnificent, and terrifying. A demon and avenging angel rolled into one. Surrounded by the glow of fox-fire, he hovered several feet off the ground, his white hair swirling around him. Unlike anything I'd ever seen before, he had tails in his human form. Four of them, three white, and one black. And ears, he had fox ears atop his head. He was more beast than man, and his fierce expression was intent on me at the moment. I didn't know what to make of the changes in him.

"Makoto? What's happening to you?"

His gaze flicked above me, his eyes glowing red. "Release her to me. She's mine."

"Mmm … what's happening to you indeed?" Prince Anyon drawled lazily. "You've become a yako kitsune fully, haven't you? And become more powerful in the process. And yet, you have three white tails, and one black. How interesting."

"Kiernan! The charm!" I scrambled forward on my hands and knees, peering down into the hole that had housed Kiernan's body. And just as I had expected, although I'd hoped otherwise, the wooden box was now empty. I had no doubt he was long gone. Which would mean Makoto's fox-fire was no longer a product of a magical boost. It was all him now.

Makoto reached out as if I was right next to him. "Rems." He said my name like a prayer.

I stood but was yanked back by my hair. "No one said you were going anywhere. Maybe Crel has forgiven you, but I haven't."

I reached up, digging my nails into the prince's slender hand. "I think you're about to have a much bigger problem than me. That charm is now in the possession of someone very dangerous. Someone who has an ax to grind with the fae." I wouldn't mention that he wasn't exactly pleased with the witches either.

"Who?"

"Kiernan, of course. The first goblin to ever exist, and the rightful goblin king."

His grip tightened in my hair. "No. He's just a rumor, a myth, a legend."

"Oh, I can assure you of his existence. He's the one who aided me in Somniare. He's the one who stole Makoto's spirit heart in order to blackmail us into finding his body. And he's the one who wanted the charm." I twisted around, defiantly raising my gaze to bore into Prince Anyon's diamond glare. "And he's the goblin who's spent centuries holding a grudge against your kind, and now he's out of his box."

Prince Anyon flung me away, gaping. "What have you done?"

"What I had to."

"And yet your kitsune seems irrevocably altered," Crel interjected.

I glanced back and forth between him and the prince. "Kiernan was still pissed about something I did to him in Somniare. He didn't give us—he didn't hold up his end of the bargain, not really." My mind conjured up the image of Makoto's pulverized heart, my chest constricting.

Prince Anyon shifted, crossing his arms over his chest. "Mmm … glad to know I'm not the only one who can't trust you."

"Please. Like I can trust you either. Fae and witches aren't friends. And we never struck a formal deal. I said I'd get the charm from Crel, which I did, and I also said I wouldn't hurt him beyond repair." I slid my gaze over Crel with meaning. "And voila, a healed Crel. You should have known better than to leave loopholes … Your Highness."

Prince Anyon tilted his head, considering. "You have me there. Even still, what you did to Crel—"

"Is no less than you would have done for me if you were in Remy's position." Crel cupped the back of Prince Anyon's neck, turning the prince to face him.

A silent conversation passed between Crel and Prince Anyon, culminating in a passionate kiss between the two males. I couldn't help but be intrigued for a moment— barely an instant in time. After all, both the prince and Crel were incredibly good-looking.

Oh, stop it. You're not a voyeur, or twelve. I was wasting the perfect opportunity to make a break for it.

I stepped to the side, warily glancing around, but all others in the field had been culled by fox-fire and were no longer any kind of threat. I sprinted for Makoto, and he shot towards me, swooping me up in his arms, his eyes shifting from red to black with his emotions.

"Put me down," I groused. "I don't need to be carried around like an invalid." He ignored me, and instead rose higher into the air, his fox-fire burning brighter.

"I *will* make it an official command."

"Just let me protect you for once."

"I don't need you to protect me." I glanced back at Crel and Prince Anyon who had advanced to PG-13 status, and I was guessing would be hitting an NC-17 rating at any moment before rolling right into R. It was exactly the over-the-top spontaneous groping that led to so many problems in real life. If not for the fact that I actually wanted to talk to the prince and Crel, it would have been the perfect moment for our complete escape.

I clapped my hands together sharply, not wanting to witness a real live sex show, no matter how attractive the subjects were. If I wanted to see porn, I'd go to the internet, where I could find any kind of fetish available. Humans excelled at making such things in abundance and easily attainable. "Hey! Stop acting like thirteen-year-old male humans!" Normally I would have said fae, but being that the prince was fae, it wasn't much of an insult.

Crel groaned, pulling his lips away from the prince's, his eyes glowing like two green flashlights. He murmured something into Prince Anyon's ear, and broke away from him, standing slowly, keeping his midsection slightly turned away. *Like I don't know what's going on down there.* I rolled my eyes.

Crel cleared his throat. "I was distracting him so you could escape. I'm guessing you have a reason for sticking around."

Prince Anyon glared at Crel, but there was no real heat in the look. "Distract me. I'll teach you the meaning of distraction later."

"Yeah, actually, I do." I pointed at the ground and jerked my head. "Makoto, put me down already."

Makoto grumbled under his breath but finally complied. He set me down softly but kept an arm wrapped around my middle, as if he couldn't bear the thought of not having some kind of contact with me. His tails twitched rapidly against the ground, which was disconcerting because of the fact that he wasn't in fox form.

"Where's Eve?" I'd almost completely forgotten about her.

Makoto leaned in to rest his chin on my shoulder. "She wasn't here when I woke up. A shame."

I rolled my eyes again, knowing damn well he couldn't care less what happened to Eve. "Yeah, whatever." As much as I liked having Eve around because of the things she represented to me, if she was missing, she'd either have to find her way back, or I'd look for her later. Now was not the time to worry about a living doll, especially one who could usually take care of herself.

I pointed at Prince Anyon, narrowing my eyes. "Are you planning on pursuing this revenge thing with me? Or are we free to go now?" It was always best to know where one stood with a fae.

"Let them go," Crel rumbled, curling a finger under Prince Anyon's chin. "We have more important things to concern ourselves with."

"Do you truly believe that a war—the big war—is right around the corner? Or was talk of that all for manipulative purposes?" I directed my question to the prince before he could even react to Crel's touch.

Prince Anyon flicked a wave of his platinum hair over his shoulder and shrugged away from Crel. "Just like a *cailleach*, never taking things seriously." He leaned forward, his expression stark. "Even if I wasn't certain before, with a wildcard such as Kiernan on the loose in possession of the charm that should be in my hands ..." He turned, cursing in fae under his breath. "We all have reason to fear now."

I read between the lines. He had been manipulating me, and now that Kiernan had the charm, the prince wasn't opposed to using me again to try and obtain said charm. I wasn't going to play his games anymore. "It'll be fine."

Just then, as if my words had conjured them, a half dozen male goblins materialized in the space between us. They were all dressed in dark colors that showed off their silver-toned skin to perfection. Beautiful, and intimidating, both in appearance and magical strength, their energy hummed along my skin, Kiernan's in particular, the sameness of it calling to me.

The prince and Crel staggered back with surprise, and Makoto expanded his fox-fire, creating a protective bubble around us.

Out from behind a rather large goblin stepped a familiar face, although a lot younger than the last time I'd seen him in Somniare. I'd sensed him, but it was still jarring for him to be so different in age physically. "You don't seem surprised to see me, "Kiernan said, his gaze locked with mine. His voice wasn't as low as I was used to hearing, but the tone and cadence both were the same.

"I had a feeling we'd be seeing you again, and soon. I was just hoping I'd be wrong."

"It didn't take you long to find your kind," Makoto added, his grip around me tightening.

Kiernan shrugged. "A king must have his subjects, after all."

"What do you want, goblin?" Prince Anyon snapped, having recovered from his shock. "Why are you here, uninvited, on Light Court land?"

"I want all of you, of course." He snapped his fingers, plunging us into darkness.

Chapter 14

"Wake up!" Ice-cold water splashed into my face, and I sputtered, jerking straight up. "What the hell?" Chains rattled when I moved, and I hastily discovered my wrists were bound in shackles that were attached to a stone wall. I clamored to my feet, staggering as I hit the end of my bindings.

"Makoto?" I swung my gaze around what appeared to be a small, dank cell. But aside from my captor, who was standing just beyond my reach, I was alone. "Where is he, Kiernan? Where's Makoto?"

Kiernan smoothed his bare hands down the front of his black tunic, and curled his fingers into his leather-clad thighs, shifting from one foot to the other. He seemed almost uncomfortable in his own body, his mannerisms plagued with nervous twitches. "Your kitsune is in another room much like this one. But on the other side of the palace. Far from you." His icy gaze studied me, waiting for my response.

"What about Prince Anyon and Crel?"

"His delightful majesty is hanging in a golden cage in my throne room. He is unharmed, yet very perturbed."

"And Crel?"

"The dragon is also in my throne room, on display."

I heaved a sigh of relief. Sure Crel and the prince weren't technically my friends, but I had a feeling I was going to need them if I was going to put a stop to Kiernan's play for power. Or at least make him leave me alone, permanently.

"Why are you doing this?"

"The goblins were very welcoming upon my arrival. Between the charm," he absently rubbed his thumb over the round disk around his neck, "and my magic, they were impressed, but what got me declared king so quickly ... I know all of their secrets." He chuckled, pacing back and forth. "I've spent centuries being able to peer into all of their heads when they slept. The amount of information I have about all of them is staggering."

"Oh, I see. Blackmail is totally your thing. But what's that got to do with Makoto and me? Huh? We've already played your game. And lost."

"I still have use for you and the kitsune. As for Prince Anyon and Crel ... the two lovebirds make fine scenery in my throne room."

"You have your body back. You're free. And a king. Plus, you have the Prince of the Light Court hanging in a cage for your amusement—what more could you want?" I wasn't sure if even Kiernan knew about the queen's demise, and if he didn't know, I wasn't going to give him any more power with that little tidbit of knowledge.

Kiernan leaned against the wall, his knee jerking sporadically. "Witches and light fae—all fae, except for goblins and other members of the Dark Court—will pay for what was done to me."

"Okay, maybe the light fae deserve it because they're so old and the ones who helped lock you away are probably alive and kicking, but you can't punish witches who weren't even born yet for something other generations did."

"I've spent centuries waiting for the opportunity to get my revenge. I care little if a few innocents suffer along with the guilty."

Yep, ladies and gents. I'm the one who released this crazy into the world. If only I had known that Makoto's spirit heart would be lost to him no matter what, I would have left Kiernan in Somniare to rot for the rest of eternity. *Stupid, stupid, stupid. Why didn't I trust my gut on that one?* But of course, I knew why. My love for Makoto was my greatest weakness—a weakness that Kiernan had attacked mercilessly. And even though I'd known it, I was helpless to defend myself against such tactics.

I crossed my arms over my chest, the edge of the manacles digging into the top part of my stomach. "You have nothing left to lord over me."

Kiernan raised his dark brows, smiling brightly like I'd

just told a joke. "And your kitsune's life isn't enough to make you do what I want?"

"Everyone knows kitsunes are damn near impossible to kill."

"Near impossible, not impossible." His eyes glinted as he tilted his head. "I can kill him," he lifted his hand to study his nails, "if I wanted to."

"You didn't exactly instill trust with your little stunt with Makoto's heart."

He shrugged. "You didn't have a choice then, and you still don't."

"Doesn't she?" Makoto stood in fox form at the entrance of the cell, its three white tails and one black waving high in the air. "You may be strong, Kiernan, and you took us all by surprise, but this isn't Somniare, a place you learned to hold dominion over."

Kiernan whirled around, golden flames shooting from his hands. Makoto leapt through the air, lightning fast, landing softly in front of me. He laughed, the multi-layered sound echoing off the walls. "Is that all you've got?"

Kiernan snarled, shooting more flames at Makoto. Fox-fire exploded around us, absorbing all of it, the scent of negative ions permeating the air. Makoto chuckled long and low. "I thought you were this master plotter. And here you went and made me stronger. As you can see, with the loss of my spirit heart, I gained my fourth tail ... again, and the power boost to go with it. Thanks for that."

My manacles clattered to the floor, partially melted by

fox-fire. I rubbed my wrists and stood. The metal had been spelled to bind my magic, and now that I was free, Makoto wasn't the only one who could fight.

I raised my hand, Tarik appearing in it, blazing a vivid red, vibrating with anger. My magical flames shot up the blade, sparks jumping off of him like tiny, angry fireflies. "You've made a big mistake, Kiernan. Big mistake. Because now I have no reason to want to keep you alive. I could solve everyone's problems with one flick of my wrist." I sliced Tarik through the air to demonstrate my intentions.

The three of us stood there, no one making the first move, three sets of eyes dancing around the room warily.

Finally, Kiernan spoke, breaking the silence. "You can't beat me. I—"

"You can't beat us either," I interjected. "I know your magic, and you know mine. Makoto as a yako kitsune is just as strong as you, even with the fae charm. Kind of sucks, doesn't it?"

"It appears we are at a stand-off," Kiernan growled, his eyes flashing with fury.

"Yep, looks that way." I patted Makoto on the head, just needing to touch my kitsune.

Makoto leaned into me, all four tails curving around my hip. "There are two of us and one of you. Plus, no one took into account Tarik. In a way, there are three of us."

"I won't let the two of you go. I've spent too long planning for all of this."

I nodded slowly. "That's very good villain speak. Next, how about you explain your entire plan, step by step? All the cool villains are doing it." I bit my lower lip to keep from laughing. Tarik was affecting my mood, as usual, making me feel almost whimsical, although what I'd said was true. Kiernan, as it turned out, had all the makings of a stereotypical villain. Instead of moving on, and simply making the best of what he could have, he would stay rooted in the past, and obsessed with his grand revenge. *Who does that ever work for? And who knew characters like Kiernan existed outside of comic books?*

"Witches, kitsunes, dragons, goblin kings, and fae princes, oh my!" Prince Anyon exclaimed from the entrance of the cell. He tapped his chin with his index finger and tilted his head. "Or is that, a witch, a kitsune, a dragon, a goblin king, and a fae prince walk into a bar?"

"Anyon," Crel chastised, coming into view.

Kiernan quickly glanced in front of himself and behind, before disappearing in a puff of gold smoke. He'd never been one to be foolish about such things, I'd give him that.

"Now," Prince Anyon regarded Makoto and me, "maybe I'm ready to have a talk with you two."

I quirked an eyebrow. "Mmm ... well, maybe I'm over you," I waved my hands around me, "and all of this." Not to mention I had the little issue of my father to deal with. Oh, and the demon I owed three ... or was it four favors to? *Crap. I need to get my shit together.*

I blinked, and the four of us were in the center of Prince Anyon's gaudy room. "No one gave you permission to bring us here!" Makoto snapped, a purple flash revealing my kitsune in her original female form. No signs of fox ears or a tail were visible. The only difference in her appearance was the darker color of her eyes.

"I'm getting a bit tired of getting 'popped' all over the place. Although," my stomach growled when I spotted a tray heaped with food sitting in the corner of the room, "I am a bit hungry." I hurried forward, drawn by the scrumptious aroma of fae food. As I stuffed my face, probably resembling a chipmunk, I wondered if one could get addicted to fae food. Until I'd seen it, I hadn't thought I was hungry. The energy I'd boosted from Alternum itself was still humming through my system. That brought up an anxious thought: *Maybe fae food was safe, but was I going to wake up every night for six months jonesing for some pink wafer things? What if I started offering sexual favors to fae for just a taste of*—I eyed a blue fluffy thing before popping it in my mouth—*whatever that was.*

Makoto leaned into me, giggling. "Don't worry, Rems. If that becomes a problem, I'll make sure I'm always stocked with pink wafer things. Or these …" She popped a blue fluffy thing in her mouth and chewed.

My cheeks heated. "What did I say about not commenting on my inner dialogue? Huh?"

She giggled again but kept anything else she was thinking to herself. *Thank the gods.*

"Whenever the two of you have had your fill …" Prince Anyon flopped down on a white couch, a look of boredom glazing over his features.

"Stop being so rude," Crel chastised him, pointedly sitting on a chaise lounge a few feet away from the prince.

"Since when are you the *cailleach*'s champion?" Prince Anyon stuck out his lower lip in a pout. "Do I have to almost burn you to death to get you to take my side for once?"

"The only side I'm taking is the right one. Don't be the spoiled brat we all know you can be."

I was surprised how Crel seemed to be the dominant one in their relationship. From what I'd heard of Prince Anyon, he was the one who usually preferred to have control of ... well, everything. *Maybe that's part of what he loves about Crel?* I didn't particularly care one way or the other about Prince Anyon, but it was interesting to see a being that I thought incapable of love, do just that—love Crel. It was obvious in the way he watched Crel, moved around him, and genuinely seemed to care for him.

I glanced over at Makoto, who was watching me. I gave her a wane smile before turning away. I was worried. As usual, I was doing a fantabulous job of locking away my feelings, or at least keeping them below the surface of my consciousness, even though I knew they were there. Plus, as a witch, having grown up around and having trained extensively to do magic, I lived in a different world than humans. Expectations of me, and how I reacted to things, were not the same. Being murdered, spending time in Somniare, being hurtled back into reality, and all the other problems that had followed me there ... None of that struck me as out of the ordinary.

Sure, my everyday life before my murder had been calmer, but not by much. Being a witch, even a Novem, meant I'd always been surrounded by risk, and had to face death at a very young age. If I panicked or worried too much, I would have had a nervous breakdown a long time ago. *Or maybe I did and just didn't realize it. Hmm ... Nah.*

Despite that, my weak spot was Makoto. All of my kitsune's original forms had shown a drastic change in personality since Kiernan stole her spirit heart. And now, suddenly, she was acting more reasonable, normal even. That almost scared me more than the rest. There were other things we had to deal with, but none of them were half as important as Makoto's wellbeing. *But now that the spirit heart is destroyed, nothing can be done.* I forced myself to swallow, the food I was eating having suddenly turned to dirt in my mouth.

Makoto prowled the length of the room and back, her long strides graceful as always. Her slender fingers trailed over various objects as she took in everything around her. My kitsune was much more observant than me. More than half the time I didn't notice my surroundings. I relied on my familiar to fill me in on things I missed. A bad habit that I'd never overcome.

Prince Anyon scowled in Makoto's direction. "Find anything you like?"

Makoto grinned. "Maybe."

I continued to watch Makoto silently, studying her for changes—wondering what it would truly mean for us now that her spirit heart was permanently gone. *She doesn't have a problem with me being a tenebris witch, or with the fact that my appearance has been slightly altered.* Maybe in the end it would be the same. Maybe Makoto becoming a yako kitsune wouldn't need more than a period of adjustment between us. After all, no matter what Makoto became, I'd always love every part of my kitsune. Every single piece, light or dark. That's what it meant to love someone. You didn't walk away when things got tough, even if they might not ever get easier again.

"Sooo ..." I moved away from the tray of food, rubbing my full belly. I raised my eyebrows at Prince Anyon. "What was it you wanted exactly?"

"Oh, just wanted to discuss the little matter of you releasing the goblin king and giving him my charm."

"I told you, I didn't have a choice."

Vivid skepticism twisted his features. "Yes, because he gave you back that heart just like he promised." He stared pointedly at Makoto, who swiped a small object off a tabletop, sliding it inside her kimono.

She glanced up, noticing three pairs of eyes on her. She smiled, and pulled the object out of her kimono, placing it back on the table. "Sorry," she muttered.

"Sorry you got caught," I grumbled. What was with her little klepto move anyways? That was new. What other little oddities could I expect to show up in the very near future?

Crel stood abruptly, stomping across the room, looming over the prince. "We're going to have a civil discussion. No more snide remarks." He bent down to brush his lips against the prince's, murmuring, "For now. Because you know how much I love that smart mouth of yours and all the things it can do."

I rolled my eyes, although curiosity got the best of me. The two of them had gotten over their little … tiff pretty quickly. Was it because the prince had been able to give Crel what he wanted? "So did you lock that down, Crel? Does Prince Anyon belong to you à la dragon style now?"

"Yes," Crel rumbled, his eyes glowing. "He's mine." He palmed the back of the prince's neck, staring into his eyes. Thankfully their conversation was private, held silently between them. I had a feeling it would have burned my ears. Plus, there is a thing as too much information.

"Huh." Makoto tilted her head, her curiosity piqued as well. "So the bond worked between two males, and one who wasn't dragon? Interesting."

Crel pulled away from Prince Anyon, settling down beside him. "My magic is strong and so is his."

I nodded. "Congrats. I'm glad that's all settled."

Crel scowled. "Not exactly. My kind aren't pleased."

"Why not?"

Prince Anyon waved his hand flippantly. "Dragons aren't as open-minded as the fae."

"Oh, so it's frowned upon in dragon culture to have same sex bondings?" It wouldn't be the first time certain species had issues with making sure gender norms were adhered to. Humans were notorious for such ludicracy.

"No." Crel ran his hand over his head. "My people have an issue with him being fae, and not dragon."

"Ridiculous, right?" The prince twirled a piece of his platinum hair around his finger. "Everyone knows the fae, especially any from the Light Court, are superior to any other species. Plus, I'm royal—about to be king in fact, not that they know that part. It's simply that Crel upgraded and they're pissed. Probably all jealous, if you ask me."

I snorted. "Yeah, okay. Moving along. What do you propose be done about Kiernan?"

The prince stared up at the ceiling, continuing to twirl his hair. "We kill him, of course. Then we get my charm back. I don't care in which order. Really, as long as it happens."

Makoto sashayed over to stand next to me, slipping something small into my hand covertly, winking. I palmed the object and tucked it into my back pocket. *Great, klepto kitsune strikes again.*

I cleared my throat hoping no one noticed the handoff between Makoto and myself. "We may have escaped from —wherever we were—goblin land, but—"

"The Dark Court," Prince Anyon supplied. "We were in the bowels of the dirty Dark Court." He feigned a shudder, swiping at his pristine white clothing.

"Okaaaay, the Dark Court, but it won't be easy to take him out," I snapped my fingers, "just like that."

"Which is why we're here. To come up with a plan," Crel offered.

"Well we haven't been doing much planning at all—"

"You're right. You've been eating, and nosing into personal things that aren't your business, and," he motioned to Makoto, "your *yako* kitsune has been pawing through my things, and helping herself to several of my favorite bobbles, I might add." He jutted an accusatory finger in her direction. "Don't think I haven't seen you."

Makoto scooted over next to me, hanging her head, although I could tell she wasn't really repentant. Again, just sorry for getting caught. I sighed. "Listen …" I rubbed my temples. "Hey, where is Eve, by the way? Is she here?" I couldn't believe I'd lost her, again. Of course, maybe now that Kiernan was free … *No.* My heart dropped into my stomach at the thought. I hadn't known what to think of the latest version of my voodoo doll, except that I wasn't ready to give her up yet. But have I seen her since—

Black smoke poured up from the ground, quickly gathering in the center of the room. I gasped, clutching at the wall behind me as two eyes, burning brightly like the ends of cigarettes, gazed at me from a formless body.

A flash of purple, and male Makoto—brandishing a glowing Tarik—lunged in front of me. In the same moment, Crel was on his feet in front of the prince, fire racing up his arms from his hands, his eyes like two green flashlights.

"I'm here for one of the favors I'm owed," the inky voice slithered around me.

I moved to step around Makoto, but he wouldn't budge. I peeked my head over his shoulder, standing on my tiptoes. "What's the favor?" I somehow managed to keep my voice steady, despite my insides quivering with fear. Demons of any kind were unknown entities by and large to me. If that wasn't the case I never would have gotten myself into the 'owing debt to a denizen of hell situation' by accident.

"You are to present yourself to Kiernan, to be delivered immediately by me."

My eyes widened. "No. No, that's not a favor. That's—"

"That is the favor I require of you. If you do not fulfill it, then I will be free to do with you whatever I wish." The shadow demon bobbed up and down, smoke rolling as if the prospect excited him.

"No, I won't go to him."

"I will also be free to slaughter the kitsune, since saving him was part of the original bargain."

My nostrils flared as I attempted to breathe evenly. Without another word or another thought, I knew I was about to do the most asinine thing of my entire life. I darted around Makoto, his clawed hand snatching at me desperately, but the strength to break his grasp was given to me by my love for him. I wouldn't allow him to be hurt one more time because of me.

The demon's body swirled around me, and I choked on the smoke, my eyes burning. "It'll be fine," I yelled. "I escaped once, and I can do it again." I wouldn't let myself think about the fact that I hadn't been alone, and I would be this time. None of that mattered. I'd find a way out, just like I always did. *All that matters is that Makoto is safe, at least for now.*

Chapter 15

I opened my eyes to the sight of bars. Golden bars ornately crafted, and bowed at the top, gathered into—

Comprehension hit me, and I lurched to my feet, my world shifting as I swung back and forth in a cage. I gripped the spelled metal, glaring down below me, knowing what I'd see. A throne room. One that was currently empty, save Kiernan's pretty new bird ... me.

No, no, no, no, no. I can't be in here. I can't be stuck in this tiny cage. My heart thrashed against my ribcage, threatening to burst. *No. Stop. You can't let this get to you. You're a strong witch. Small spaces aren't a big deal. You can handle this. And you'll get out soon.* At least I hoped.

I forced myself to breathe normally, my eyes darting around the surroundings outside my prison. I'd only been in the Light Court's throne room once when I was a little witchling, but it had left a lasting impression.

Everything in it was white and gold, the décor gaudy, much like Prince Anyon's private chambers. Marble polished floors had shone like mirrors, beautiful fae creatures danced and laughed in every corner. It was everything human children would expect from a fairy tale, even the subtle dangerous edge from the original tales.

The Dark Court was the polar opposite. The throne room was dark, utilitarian. The floors were black, the surface dull, as if it absorbed light instead of reflecting it. The décor was ... lacking, if there was any at all. Everything was either black or grey, except the throne itself, if you could call it that, which sat directly below me, a large silver chair with no padding of any kind. It was all a bit depressing in some odd way.

The large black double doors creaked open, and Kiernan strode in, his icy eyes locked onto me, a smile curling his lips. Without a word he went to his throne and sat, staring straight ahead.

I shook the bars, causing the cage to swing again. "Hey! Hey asshat! Let me out of here now!"

He cleared his throat, and shifted, getting comfortable.

"I said to let me out of here!" Anger boiled my blood, flushing my face. "I swear I'm going to rip you limb from limb with my bare hands, no magic necessary, when I get out of here."

His only response was a low chuckle.

"You think this is funny?" Of course he did. He was obviously doing everything for my benefit, to get more of a rise out of me. The problem was, despite me knowing that, I couldn't contain my rage.

He cleared his throat and spoke loudly, "That cage is spelled. While you're in it, you won't require food, or need to tend to any other bodily needs."

What? He plans on leaving me in here without any kind of reprieve at all? Even birds get let out sometimes, don't they? The golden bars seemed to flex, shrinking around me. Instead of panicking again like I thought I would, a wave of exhaustion hit me and I flopped down, crossing my legs. The cage wobbled a bit before settling. I dipped my fingers underneath me, reaching into my pocket to produce the small object Makoto had given me. It looked like a marble, the glass warm from being close to my skin. I palmed it, wishing Makoto was with me. "Why are you doing this? Any of this? It can't really be about what I did to you in Somniare?" *Can it?*

Kiernan tilted his head back, looking up at me. I propped my elbows on my knees, glaring down at him. He quirked a dark eyebrow. "Does it matter?"

He was right. I didn't care why he was doing it, just that he stopped messing with me and mine. I decided to cut to the chase. "What do you really want? Because I don't think it's me in a cage."

"Of course not. Although," he grinned, "I am enjoying the sight of you in that cage. I think you may be my favorite thing about the Dark Court now."

"What do you want?" I growled from between clenched teeth.

"I want what's mine."

"You have the Dark Court throne, and you have your body back, what else is there?" His lips pressed into a thin line and he dropped his head. "What else is there?" I pressed.

"I may have the throne, and I'm surrounded by my kind for the first time in my life ... but I'm not satisfied." His fingers curled, digging into his thighs. "I want what I should have had. I want what's mine by all rights."

"You're not making a whole lot of sense. Is it the teenage hormones? I mean, I know you're centuries old up here," I tapped my temple, "but your body is what? Eighteen, nineteen?" I squinted at him as he raised his head, studying his young features, which were completely disproportionate to the content in his eyes. Goblins were all stunning, their rugged beauty an antithesis to their light fae cousins, but Kiernan was even more beautiful than most. *It's a shame he's such an asshat.*

"Maybe you just need a girlfriend?" When his face twisted with anger, I tacked on, "Or boyfriend? Or both? I'm thinking the drop back into the teenage you body has made you a bit crazy. You need something to focus on besides mayhem and destruction."

"You volunteering?"

I choked on my own spit, lurching back in the cage. "No! Makoto—Makoto is the only one I want ... could ever want." The thought of my kitsune twisted my gut. He had to be going insane not being able to get to me.

Kiernan tapped his chin. "I really thought without the

spirit heart, your kitsune would have become too much for even you."

My eyes widened. "Y-you can't mean— I didn't think —" I was horrified. I had to be misinterpreting what he was saying. Had to be.

My mind snagged on some things Kiernan had said to me in Somniare …

"Would it be so bad to be with someone like me? I could guarantee your first time would be pleasurable."

"People's dreams can reveal a lot about their true selves, and I've been watching yours for some time now."

"I'm the one who gave you the ability to send yourself here to begin with. In essence, I saved your life that time, too."

Had Kiernan, a lonely outcast, somehow come to fixate on me? Was it because I was the descendant of the only one who had ever shown him kindness before he'd been betrayed and locked away? Those who had imprisoned him never intended for his spirit to find a home in Somniare. They'd merely meant to work the loophole of the command to not actually kill him. He was to be forgotten for good. Not dead, and yet not a threat anymore. *Gods, knowing that, I almost feel sorry for him. Almost.*

"Don't worry your pretty little head, *cailleach*. I can see the wheels turning. Although I wouldn't be opposed to you using your … how do I put this? Your feminine wiles in an attempt to petition for your freedom, none of what's happened has been about you. You merely happened to be in the wrong place at the wrong time and a means to an end. Horrible luck, really."

"Then why am I here? Again, I'll ask what do you want from me?"

He stood abruptly, casting a malevolent glare my way. "I want you to shut up. *Cailleaches* are meant to be seen and not heard." He waved his hand, golden magic shimmering over me, causing the small hairs on my body to rise.

I gaped when I looked down the line of my body, inhaling the scent of Kiernan's wild magic in the process. "You—you—you stupid goblin!" I fisted the skirt on the ridiculously fancy gown Kiernan had magicked me into. It was something right out of my worst nightmares. Of course he would know. The thing was big, puffy, and pink. I looked like a living cupcake. The bell of the skirt made it so I didn't have any room to move in the cage at all. And the tiny bauble that I'd been holding was gone. The loss of it made me feel even farther from Makoto, my stomach roiling with dread.

"What?" Kiernan cupped both of his hands to his ears. "I can't hear you."

"Let me out of here and take this damn thing off of me!" I screeched.

"Why yes, my pretty little *cailleach*, you do look stunning in that dress. I'm so glad you love it. I can't wait for all those who enter this room to enjoy the sight of you as much as I do."

He strode towards the door, pausing at the threshold

of the room, glancing over his shoulder to deliver me a dazzling smile. "In case you haven't figured it out, I put a soundproof spell on the cage. No one will ever hear you scream."

I blinked, processing his words long after he disappeared from my view. Despite them, I opened my mouth and screamed, long and loud, until my voice gave out. Not that it mattered, because apparently no one but me could hear.

ℛ.

I WAS PRETTY sure I was in hell. I gripped the skirt of the pink taffeta monstrosity and turned towards the back of the room, not wanting to see those who stared at me with laughter in their eyes.

Kiernan was currently holding 'court', which he had been for the past few hours, if not an eternity, although I was pretty sure he'd just been parading goblins and other various dark fae to get a good look at me in all of my pink splendor. I had absolutely no way of knowing since he'd temporarily blocked me from hearing anything that was going on outside the cage. I was left to silently take in the taunting expressions and gestures of jeer. Which was why I was facing, for all intents and purposes, the wall.

I had so many questions and nothing to do but think. Kiernan hadn't given me any real information, of course I hadn't even gotten to ask him most of what I wanted to know. Some things I could guess at—like he obviously had some kind of control, or bargain struck with the smoke demon who he'd sent to fetch me, using the guise of one of the favors I owed the demon—but I was left with uncertainty about whether or not Kiernan had set the rest of it up. Had he somehow arranged for me to be put in the situations where I'd have to owe the demon favors, or had he stumbled upon that information later?

The cage tilted and I slid back, the puffy skirt keeping me from banging my head on the bars. I turned awkwardly to stare into an unknown species of fae's face. It was about the size of a toddler, with large gossamer, black wings. Its chubby hands gripped the bars as he rocked the cage, his cherub face twisted into a sneer.

Without thinking, I leaned forward and bit one of his fingers. He jerked away, tumbling end over end through the air before righting himself. I crossed my arms over my chest and quirked an eyebrow in challenge. I may not be able to do much inside the spelled cage, but if some tiny childlike creature wanted to mess with me—I'd bite his friggin' fingers off.

I watched as Kiernan stood, motioning to me with a grin, before he tilted his head back and laughed. The small fae joined along after a moment and flitted away to rejoin his friends on the ground, all of them laughing at my expense.

"I don't know if you can hear me in any way, Kiernan, but I will make you pay for this, I swear it. For this and for everything else you've done."

Kiernan glanced my way, his icy gaze locking with

mine for a moment before he averted his attention. I rocked back on my heels with surprise. *He can hear me.*

"Listen to me, you stupid goblin, let me go, now. Or I swear ..." And then it suddenly hit me. I was going about it all wrong. I had a tendency to be pigheaded and stubborn. I always tried to force my will upon others, instead of coercing and cajoling. The female side of Makoto had tried to teach me that you caught more bees with honey, but I'd always preferred his male side of pushing through challenges better. I'd tried one approach, to no avail. It was time to try the more manipulative angle.

I sagged, letting my knees buckle. I sank down amid my pink nightmare, the ginormous skirt sucking me down into it, creating a sort of circular pillow. Covering my face with my hands, I inhaled a shuddery breath. *I need to cry. Real tears will work best.* But I wasn't the best actress, not really. I was the brutally honest type, which was why I preferred to use direct methods, but beggars couldn't be choosers.

Just think of something you've been genuinely sad about. I immediately thought of my sister, Callie, and how she'd been brutally murdered by our father. I remembered sitting on her bedroom floor and watching her, wanting so badly to be just like her when I grew up. I devoured any and all attention she would give me. Even the smallest hint of a smile thrown in my direction made me feel so special ... loved. I'd been positive my sister was the most amazing person in all of existence. And even though it'd been obvious since day one that my magic was stronger than hers, of who I'd be in Domus Novem, she'd never once been jealous, only supportive.

Callie had contacted me from the past, knowing that she'd be murdered, just to warn me about our father, and the power that now existed within me. She'd always been selfless, the best sister anyone could ever ask for—and she was forever lost to me. And not just her, my entire family. Domus Novem was extinct. Wiped from this world. Well, all except me, and I had no idea if I had a future either.

I let all of my trials and tribulations since being murdered by my own mother wash over me, too. I'd cost Makoto the spirit heart needed to give my kitsune balance. Not only that, but I'd lost ... I'd lost so much, and I hadn't let myself feel any of it. Not really.

Hot tears—real tears—burned a path from the corners of my eyes down my face, dripping from my chin onto my gown. I sniffled, and gasped for air, my chest too tight, a lump forming in my throat. *Even if I get out of here, I can't get any of those things back. I can't bring ... back ... the ... dead.*

Or can I?

My heart thundered in my chest, my sobs growing more agitated now that the dam of my emotions had been broken. But amid my grief, amid my pathetic attempt to garner sympathy from Kiernan, a plan began to form.

And it was a gloriously stupid plan. But everyone knows, the best ones always are.

Chapter 16

I groaned, rubbing my gritty eyes with the backs of my hands. My entire face felt puffy and swollen, sore, as if someone had worked me over with their fists. I must have cried myself to sleep, although I didn't remember it … exactly. I groaned again, hating that my efforts to garner sympathy, to appear vulnerable, hadn't—

"*Cailleach*," Kiernan rumbled, as something cool and damp dropped onto my forehead.

It worked! My tears had absolutely worked! I internally did a little jig and bit the inside of my cheek to keep from smiling. I was pretty sure human feminists would have been affronted by my little show, but power is power, and I wasn't picky about how I got it, as long as I had it. *And clearly tears are their own brand of magic.* "What happened?" I croaked, my voice rough and scratchy.

"Apparently not all in my court were fans of my pet

being on display as you were, especially when you turned on the waterworks."

I peeled my eyes open, the light causing me to wince. After a moment, I sat up on my elbows, a damp washcloth sliding from my forehead to plop into my lap. I surveyed my surroundings with relief. *No more cage.* The band around my chest loosened. I was in a large room, just as dully decorated as the Dark Court throne room, everything black and grey. Still in the pink monstrosity, I lay on a large comfortable bed, which was covered with black sheets. Kiernan stood beside me, arms crossed. "I couldn't take being in there anymore." I tugged at the skirt. "This thing needs to come off. It's a torture device."

"Unless you want to be naked, it's not coming off." Kiernan's jaw muscles popped with agitation.

I sucked in a shaky breath, forcing my lower lip to tremble. "Please."

He rolled his eyes. *I can't believe he actually rolled his eyes at me.* "I said not all in my court were fans, not that I wouldn't have happily left you where you were. I'm not the fool you think I am. I know you, Remy. I've—"

"Yeah, yeah," I huffed. "Been in my dreams. Whatever. So you're planning on putting me back in there?" It wasn't an act when my heart quadrupled in time and sweat gathered around my hairline. Being stuck in that cage was a sure recipe for insanity. I wasn't good in confined spaces, something I was sure Kiernan knew.

"No. I may be king, but I'm not welcomed by all, at least not yet. I need to gain respect and support at court.

Not all dark fae hate witches. Some even like them. And to many, you are just a child. Many fae, light and dark, have a soft spot for children of all races."

I thought of all the taunting faces. "Could have fooled me. And hey, I'm not a child."

"No," he leaned into me, tracing a finger down my cheek, "you are not." I snapped at his finger, just missing it. "Better watch those teeth, *cailleach*. Some creatures bite back."

I attempted to pull magic up within me, testing whether I had access to it again since I was outside the spelled cage. When nothing came, frustration and confusion warred. *What the hell?*

Kiernan pressed his lips together, barely containing a smile, his eyes dancing with mirth. "Did you think it would be that easy?" His expression dropped into serious lines. "I don't trust you. I didn't bring you here unprepared."

"What did you do?" I ran my hands over my arms, through my hair, checking for charms, amulets, anything he could have attached to me to dampen my use of magic.

"This entire room is spelled to prevent you from using your magic." His arms rose, and he turned in a circle. "This is your new bigger cage."

"Your room?" I squeaked.

He smirked. "Enemies closer and all of that."

"Magic or not, I'll rip your balls off if you lay a hand on me."

The corner of his smirk curled into a grin. "I wouldn't

dream of it." He clomped across the floor, pausing at the door. "Now, there's someone I want you to meet."

He swung the heavy grey door open, and in marched a tall, slender female wearing a purple and black kimono. Her hair was long, hanging halfway down her back, the midnight strands lustrous and thick. She moved with supernatural grace as she neared me, her dark eyes glittering with interest. She was absolutely stunning, and her magic, the buzz of it against my skin was familiar and foreign at the same time.

"This is Akira," Kiernan said, shutting the door softly.

"Yeah, and I care because?"

Kiernan laughed. "Because this is the kitsune who will steal Makoto from you."

"Kitsune?" I sprung off the bed, tripping over my massive skirt, landing in a heap at Akira's feet. I'd never seen another kitsune before. She looked nothing like Makoto's original female self. The only thing that tied them together in any way was that they both seemed to prefer to wear kimonos, a nod to their Japanese origins. Of course, a lot of Japanese humans had at one point or another, too.

She gazed down her nose at me with disdain. "This is the witch who has the love of one of my kind?" She shook her head. "Young kitsunes are such fools."

"But you'll remedy that soon enough. Won't you, Akira?" Kiernan's icy gaze met mine with challenge.

Akira nodded her head once. "Yes. Young Makoto has never been with another kitsune. Once both sides have experienced a true blending with one of like spirit, Makoto would never choose such a lowly creature." She sneered at me. "Of course, I can understand why you'd desire a kitsune, for we are perfect, beyond all others in existence."

I realized I'd been sitting on the floor at her feet, gawking. I struggled to think of something to say, yet words escaped me. *Makoto would never leave me. Both sides of my kitsune, male and female, love me. And I love every part of Makoto. We're bonded. Nothing, not even this beautiful, stunning ... flawless kitsune could take Makoto from me.* I gulped.

But you haven't bonded as mates. My blood roared through my body as my heart sped to a gallop. And how much of Makoto had changed since becoming a yako kitsune that I didn't know about? I'd been waiting for the other shoe to drop, maybe Akira was that shoe.

"Ah, I can see the panic taking form in your eyes." Akira leaned down and curled a finger under my chin, smiling wickedly. "Don't worry, little witchling, I can promise Makoto will enjoy every minute I spend with him … and her."

I slapped her hand away, my nostrils flaring. "Makoto will never touch you. We love each other."

"One witch could never satisfy a being such as a kitsune. Tell me," she pursed her lips, her dark eyes swirling, "which side of Makoto do you prefer?"

I shifted to my knees, and then awkwardly stood, my

gown almost taking me to the floor again. I met Akira's gaze head-on. "I want them both. I'm bi-sexual."

She tilted her head. "Interesting. I understand ... a bit more now. But it's still not enough."

"Who are you to decide? Why do you even care?"

"Why do I care?" Akira's lips curled back from her teeth, sharp canines flashing. "No kitsune should ever be a servant of any kind. When Kiernan informed me of the role Makoto has been forced into—a witch's familiar—I made it my business to care."

"He's not actually my familiar. We're partners ... a team. I love him—her—all of Makoto." I refused to be intimidated by some random kitsune.

Throwing her head back, she laughed. "Okay, well none of what I said is true." A flash of purple and an all-black fox with white-tipped ears stood in front of me. Nine tails swished up into the air, also tipped in white. In a multi-layered voice, Akira added, "I'm a yako kitsune, just like the newly transformed Makoto, and I'm looking for a mate. Not many yako kitsunes are around anymore, so I've decided I want Makoto for mine." She paused. "Or maybe none of that is true either. Maybe I just enjoy causing trouble. After all, isn't that what's said about the yako?"

I growled under my breath, not sure what to believe. "You haven't even met Makoto, and you have nine tails! Makoto only has four! Your power levels don't match! And—and ..." I was grasping at straws. "You're old, Makoto is a young kitsune. Leave things alone. We match, you don't."

Akira laughed again, the sound causing all the hair on my body to rise. "Silly witch, none of that matters. I have set my sights on Makoto, and I shall possess."

Does that mean she really does want Makoto for a mate, or is Akira enjoying messing with my mind ... or both?

Kiernan opened the door, as if he'd been cued by Akira, and the black fox pranced out, tails waving in the air. "Tah-tah, witch. I'm looking forward to getting to know my future mate."

When the door was shut, Kiernan turned to me, and I flew at him, hands curled into claws. He deftly caught me, restraining me by twisting my arms behind my back. I cursed him in every language I knew, and then I made up some new words to insult him. Some very creative words. He dragged me across the floor, flinging me back on the bed when we were close enough.

I peered up at him from beyond the mass of material that made up my dress, fighting to sit up, my chest heaving. Without a word, he waved his hand, a golden swirl of magic forming a picture at the end of the bed. My breath caught when I realized it was an image of Makoto ... no, not just an image, it was Makoto, and he was—

"Let me know if you want popcorn," Kiernan said, his tone filled with amusement. Then he disappeared, leaving me alone with what I was positive was a real time peek into what was happening with Makoto.

I reached out a hand, running my fingertips through the air, wanting to touch him. His brow was furrowed, his eyes wild and panicked. Tarik was gripped tightly in his hands, glowing a bright red.

In front of Makoto stood Crel, his eyes blazing neon green. "Stop, Makoto. He's only trying to help."

"I have to get her back. Who knows— I can feel her pain, I can feel it! Who knows what's being done to her."

Prince Anyon tried to step out from around Crel but was corralled with little effort on Crel's part. "You can't go in there by yourself to get her. You have to wait," Prince Anyon called over Crel's shoulder.

A fae guard in full armor appeared to the side, tension in his face. "Your majesty, there is a—a kitsune asking specifically to see him." The guard nodded in Makoto's direction. "He claims he's here to help."

"No!" I yelled at the image. "Turn him away. Don't see him!"

"A kitsune." Makoto lowered Tarik, his expression bewildered. "Here? To see me?"

Ignoring Makoto, the guard addressed the prince again. "What should I do, my liege?"

"Send him in immediately," Prince Anyon said.

"No! You stupid fae asshat! Wrong answer!"

It was in that moment, that I realized exactly what Kiernan's new torture for me was. Or maybe it'd been the same from the beginning. After all, he'd been the one to rip Makoto's spirit heart out of his chest in Somniare. Then he attempted to imprison the both of us. Now he wanted me to watch as another kitsune tried to steal away the one person in all of the realms that I loved.

My gaze swung back and forth between Makoto, Crel, and Prince Anyon as he moved into view. *Wait. We weren't the only ones Kiernan sought to imprison.* He'd taken Crel and the prince as well. It wasn't just about Makoto and me. Kiernan seemed to be focused on couples—couples that had a chance at happiness.

But why? Why did he care about any of us? Unless … *I want what's mine.* His words echoed in my head, as I tried to unravel their true meaning.

Try as I might, none of it made any more sense than the first time he'd said it. *Think, Remy, think.*

"Makoto."

My gaze lifted back to the image, my heart stuttering. Akira entered the frame, and I couldn't look away.

Chapter 17

Makoto shifted, his gaze wary as Akira approached him in his male form. Akira, much like Makoto, wore a kimono in both male and female form, sized to fit. Akira was taller, larger, and more masculine than Makoto, I was guessing because he was older than my kitsune.

A flash of purple revealed Akira in her female form. She sashayed around Makoto in a wide circle, her gaze studying and assessing. Makoto turned with her, not giving her his back at any point. *Good. He doesn't trust Akira.*

"You've come to see me, about what?" Makoto snapped. Tarik's color changed to a golden glow, which I knew meant he wasn't ready to attack but was still alert.

"I've come to help," Akira purred.

Back off, bitch! Makoto is mine! I fisted my dress, wanting to scream.

AVA WIXX

"Why?" Makoto demanded, voice tight.

Akira lifted her shoulder in a dainty shrug. "Because you need it."

"Can you help me get back my—my witch?"

"If that's what you want."

Makoto's eyes narrowed as he raised Tarik a few inches. "How?"

"Two kitsunes are better than one. At least talk with me before you send me on my way."

"Go," Crel suggested. "What will it hurt?"

Prince Anyon nodded in agreement, his gaze sliding over Akira with suspicion of his own. "You may use the room next to this one. Find us when you're done."

Akira closed the gap between her and Makoto, wrapping her arm around one of his. "Come. Let's get to know each other and see how we might be of ... service to each other."

Tarik disappeared, and Makoto strode out of the room with Akira, his body rigid. But the picture didn't follow them, it stayed focused on the door after they left.

If she touches him, or if he touches her—if any part of Akira touches, like really touches, either form of Makoto—I'll tear that kitsune apart. And—and I'll make a coat out of her luxurious black fur. I've always looked good in black, after all.

I'd never felt so ... I struggled to put a label on it at first, but I knew deep down what it was. I was jealous. I was seething with the emotion. My skin was too tight and hot, my chest constricted, and a sick feeling—nausea mixed with a dull ache—had taken up residence in my gut.

Plus, the images, the horrifying, unwanted images of Makoto and Akira together—like really together —naked—

I ripped at my hair and screamed, needing a release of some sort. The result was unsatisfactory, fixing nothing.

Okay. Okay. Okay. Think, Remy. Just think.

Makoto's voice rose up within my mind, as memories washed over me, or at least pieces of them.

"You gave up a tail for me?"

"Anything. I would do anything for you."

"I love you with everything I am."

My eyes fluttered shut as his lips pressed to the center of my neck, air escaping his nostrils, tickling me. His tongue snaked out, tasting my skin, and then slid up along my jaw, where he nipped at my earlobe. I fisted my hands at my sides, wanting him to have control, but craving it in part myself.

"I love you, Rems. And I'll never push you away again." His *hot breath skittered along my cheek, warming me, and eliciting goose bumps.*

Confidence in the bond between Makoto and myself surged within me, lightening my mood. I'd had a moment of doubt, a twinge of jealousy. Some of it came from the fact that Makoto and I hadn't shared much of a physical relationship, besides a few kisses and some hot n' heavy grope sessions. None of that mattered though. Not really. I knew the truth. I knew what was between us. Love. True love. As corny as it sounded—even to me. But it was the truth, and love binds for all eternity. If you can walk away, it wasn't real love, at least not the soul-deep kind. Makoto and I may not have bonded as mates ... yet, but that didn't matter. Our souls were already twined in a way that could never be undone. We belonged to each other, and nothing and no one could ever come between us.

Akira's seduction attempts would be laughable.

I trust you, Makoto. I will always trust you no matter what.

I flopped back on the bed, closing my eyes. I needed some rest, despite the less-than-optimal situation I was in. Then I would refine my plans.

Everything's going to be fine. You'll find a way out of this mess just like you always do.

SUCCESS ISN'T MEASURED by how many times you fall, as long as you keep getting back up, keep trying. *One time— one chance. All I need is one chance. Just one.*

I'd failed repeatedly at besting Kiernan. Over and over I found myself with him in the power position, but that didn't mean I was going to give up. I'd never give up. *I'd rather die on my feet than live on my knees.*

I tore at the skirt on my gown, ripping off another large piece, discarding it on the floor with the heap of material that was already there. *How many damn layers does this thing have?* I'd fallen asleep quickly, remaining in a dreamless slumber for long enough to gain some focus. When I'd awoken, things had seemed ... clearer, and my determination had been rejuvenated.

I glanced up at the image hovering at the foot of the

bed. It was still focused on the door, just as it had been when Akira and Makoto had left Prince Anyon's room. I took it as a good sign that it hadn't moved. There was nothing to show, just like I knew there wouldn't be.

Akira was a fool, and so was Kiernan for that matter, if they thought such a simple thing could come between my kitsune and me. I still hadn't figured out why Kiernan seemed dead set on causing problems between certain couples though. *Maybe it doesn't really matter why, just as long as I know it's happening.*

I also wasn't sure how much control, if any, Kiernan had over the smoke demon who I owed two more favors to. It may be that they'd merely struck up a deal as well. That information, or lack of it, did matter, especially because of what I was about to do.

I stood in the middle of Kiernan's stark chamber, in my tattered dress, which I'd fashioned into pants, sort of. Okay, maybe shorts. It at least wasn't a cumbersome, gigantic pink gown anymore. I didn't care what it looked like, as long as I had freedom of movement and wasn't naked.

I clawed at the fleshy part of my left hand's palm, trying to break the skin. Pain pinched the surface of my flesh, but no blood bloomed. I growled in frustration. I used my teeth next, tearing with my canines, again to no avail. *Damnit! Why am I always getting cuts and scrapes just from existing and now that I need some blood I can't get any?* I dropped to my knees, searching for a seam in the floor, a sharp edge ... something. But the smooth black marble posed no danger to my delicate flesh, unfortunately.

I stood, prowling the room. The bed posts also had rounded edges, and were thick, leaving me no way of breaking them without the use of my magic. *Damnit! Damnit! Damnit!*

Plan B, I guess.

I chomped down on the side of my tongue, the sharp pain zinging through my mouth, the flavor of rusty pennies rolling over my taste buds. It was the obvious choice from the beginning, but such a wound was like a paper cut. Slow to heal, and annoying, even though it was minor. I would have preferred to draw my blood in another manner, but I'd run out of choices.

I shoved my fingers into my mouth, dropping back to my knees. Drawing the symbols quickly, I summoned the smoke demon mentally, focusing my energy on contacting him. *Please work without my magic. Let the symbols be enough.*

Black smoke poured up from the floor, congealing in the vague shape of the demon, its burning eyes watching me without emotion. "So eager to owe me yet another favor?"

"Do you have a deal with Kiernan or does he have dominion over you in some way?" I immediately blurted out.

The demon bobbed up into the air, hovering above me. "No one holds dominion over one such as me. No one."

"So what's your deal then? Tell me."

"No."

"Is there some kind of confidentiality thing when it comes to that kind of stuff?"

He chuckled long and low. "No such thing exists. I simply choose not to tell you for my own reasons."

"Fine, whatever." I crossed my arms over my chest. "I want to make a deal with you, too, then."

"And what possibly do you have that I would want? You already owe me the sum of three favors again."

"Would you have use for a yako kitsune's tails? Say nine of them?"

The demon swayed in front of me, his burning eyes level with mine. "A yako kitsune's tails are very powerful." He was silent a moment. "I could make use of them. What would be your terms?"

"I get you the tails, and we're even, no more favors. But first, you get me out of here, take me back to the Light Court."

"Done."

"I wasn't finished." The demon grunted, so I continued, "You get the fae charm back from Kiernan, and while you're at it—put his spirit back in Somniare. Oh, and then—"

"I will free you, take you to the Light Court, and I will consider your favors, all three of them, paid in full. That is what I will give you in exchange for the nine tails."

"You'd have to free me, and take me to the Light Court before I can deliver you the tails."

"You have forty-eight hours from the time I free you

for the deal to expire. Then I will bring you back here, and you will owe me nine favors."

"Nine?" I squeaked. *I knew it. Demons are the loan sharks of the underworld.*

"One for each tail you failed to deliver."

I nibbled on my thumbnail. Is this really what I wanted? What if I couldn't get the tails? Or worse, what if guilt clawed its way to the surface like it had with Miles? I couldn't blame Akira for her wanting Makoto. I actually wasn't targeting her because of it either. *Okay, maybe a little.* She simply had the only thing I could think to offer a demon for a bargain ... that I could bear to part with.

I snapped my fingers, my thumb slick from me chewing on it. "Oh, and you won't try to collect any of the prior favors until the forty-eight hours is up. It would kind of make it difficult if Kiernan sent you to fetch me again."

"That is agreeable."

"It's a deal then. I will give you nine yako kitsune tails by the end of forty-eight hours, as counted in Mundi, the human realm, the clock beginning from the time of my freedom, in exchange for you taking me to the Light Court, and considering all favors paid in full upon receipt of said tails. Failure to deliver on my side of the bargain at the expiration of forty-eight hours will result in me owing you nine favors in total."

I smiled when the demon bobbed up and down, obviously displeased that I'd caught on to the fact that he was planning on tacking nine more favors onto the three I already owed him if I didn't deliver. Not that it mattered much, since if I ended up owing him nine favors, I was screwed. Three more wouldn't make me any less so.

"Deal," he finally said, "I accept your terms."

"Well, yippee skippee." *Score one for me! Kiernan like ten, and me ... one. Still, sometimes all you need is one to get back in the game.*

Chapter 18

Smoke surrounded me—I was weightless, blind—all of my senses submerged.

"The forty-eight Mundi hours begin now," the demon's voice slithered through my mind.

The inside of my right wrist burned, and I flailed, still no sense of anything around me.

Suddenly color and sound exploded around me, disorientation causing me to stumble, and I grabbed wildly at anything to give me purchase.

"Remy?" I blinked Prince Anyon's face into focus, realizing I was clinging to his arm. "How did you get here?"

"Set her down over here," Crel grated, his tone agitated.

"How long until you reign this in, Crel? I find I cannot stand your jealousy."

"It's the *Anam Cara* bond. I rationally know that her touching you is—just step away from her!"

"Makoto?" I croaked, glancing down at my wrist. The number 2880 was scrolled across my skin like a tattoo. It changed to 2879 before my eyes. It took me a second to register that the demon had given me a countdown clock … in my flesh. *Fabulous.*

Prince Anyon did what Crel asked, and stepped away from me. He was wearing only a loose pair of white pants, his hair unfastened, and cascading around his shoulders. Crel was adorned in similar attire, only black.

My cheeks heated with sudden realization. "Oh, um … Sorry." I'd obviously interrupted something. You would think the demon would have dropped me off closer to Akira—being it was her tails I was after—and not in the private chambers of Prince Anyon and his new mate. I wondered for a moment if they'd been dressed when I'd first been dumped into Alternum, or if they had dressed really, really fast while I had been blind to them.

I glanced over at Crel who had curled his arm around the prince's waist protectively, tucking him into his side. His expression was relaxed, as if the contact between the two of them grounded him. *I know the feeling, buddy, which is why I need to find Makoto like yesterday.*

"Now that Crel is done acting crazy." Prince Anyon smirked up at Crel, tapping his nose playfully. "I can ask—where have you been, and what are you wearing?"

I pinched the bridge of my nose, counting back from ten slowly. "Please tell me while I was off being tortured by Kiernan, the two of you weren't rolling around in bed together. Please tell me you were thinking of ways to rescue me."

Both Prince Anyon and Crel had the good sense to bow their heads sheepishly. The prince lifted his gaze to mine, peeking up through his platinum lashes. "But you obviously saved yourself. See, there was no need to worry."

Unbelievable. I'd at least thought Prince Anyon—no, I knew I could only count on Makoto. I'd accepted that long ago. What the prince and Crel had been doing was of no concern of mine.

"How long has Makoto been with Akira?"

Crel and Makoto glanced at each other, the prince clearing his throat. "How do you know about Akira?"

"Don't ask me that. Just tell me— Never mind. Point me in the direction of where I can find them."

"You might not want to—"

I quirked a brow, instantly shutting Crel up. "I trust Makoto. If that dumb yako kitsune thinks for one second that it can steal my Makoto with something as simple as seduction ..." I snorted. "It's just not going to happen. Now, which way?" I growled.

"The next room over," Prince Anyon responded. "But they have been in there quite a while." He winced as if I would lose my mind just from finding that out.

"Mmm hmm ... the thing is, Makoto isn't a commitment-challenged fae. He can be alone in a room with someone and not ... well, you know!" I whirled around, stalking from the room. A buzz of magic rolled down my body, and I was back in my black tank top, black pants, and black motorcycle boots. I was fairly certain I'd been magically bathed as well.

"You're welcome," Prince Anyon called.

He didn't do anything except give me directions, and a bit of magic which I could have done myself if I'd wanted. *Stupid fae.* "I'm not thanking you."

"You never do."

Grumbling under my breath, I made my way to the next room over from Prince Anyon's personal chambers. I kicked the pristine white door open, the heavy wood flying back to hit the wall.

My heart stuttered to a stop, all oxygen leaving my lungs. *No.*

There in a large bed, was the male version of Makoto … naked, with an equally bare female Akira curled around him. She lifted her head, her dark eyes glittering with triumph. Makoto didn't stir, his chest rising and falling in the even pattern of sleep.

No. It—no.

I couldn't move, couldn't breathe, couldn't— *How could he? How could any part of Makoto betray me this way? What's it been, a few hours? And he knew I was being held captive by Kiernan. I was being held captive by Kiernan and he was— he was—*

False. This is false, a voice floated across my mind. It was so tiny, I hardly noticed it behind the rage welling up within me. But I did hear it. Somehow it whittled its way past my consciousness, demanding my attention, which is when I realized it was my witch's intuition, something I'd learned to trust above all other things.

I inhaled a shuddering breath. "This is false," I declared with certainty. "Makoto would never betray me. Never."

Akira's lips pressed together in a thin line, her nails lengthening to claws as she moved her hand down Makoto's defined chest. "Oh, but he did. And she did. Makoto belongs to me now."

I sniffed the air, a bitter taste, like burnt toast settling on my tongue. "You lie. I can taste your foul magic." I wiggled my fingers, knowing what I had to do. "Tarik, I need you." I grinned when he popped into my hand, glowing a vibrant red, as ready as I was for attack.

Akira sat up, hissing, "Makoto's katana answers to you?"

I gripped the base of Tarik tightly with both hands, shuffling forward a few steps. "Of course he does. Makoto and I belong to each other. We share everything."

"But not a physical relationship."

"Not yet." I flicked my gaze to Makoto's passive face, his body completely motionless. "Now, remove whatever spell you've placed on Makoto, before—"

Akira was on her feet in an instant, a flash of purple revealing the male version of her brandishing his own katana. Nine tails plumed out behind him, and black fox ears with white tips were flattened against his head. "Once you're dead, Makoto will eventually move on, with me!"

"Not happening," I grunted, lifting Tarik higher as I

ran at Akira. My magic shot from my palms morphing into flames, rushing up the blade, red sparks dripping down. I gritted my teeth, determination surging through me, the emotion so strong it overrode Tarik's. Or maybe we simply felt exactly the same in that moment, both of us needing to protect Makoto more than anything else.

Akira swung first, the contact of our swords clanging together jarring, my jaw aching. I managed to hold my ground, not giving an inch. Our gazes locked over the blades for a moment, hate flying between us. I spun away, pivoting back to swipe below his defenses. He moved to counter, blocking my attack with ease.

"I'm stronger than you," he growled. "Give up now and I'll make your death quick, honorable."

"Ditto, but in reverse."

He snarled, rapidly hitting down on Tarik with his sword, the fighting style akin to someone using a claymore or a broadsword as opposed to a katana. I'd been taught to use agility and speed, which was what a katana was suited for, the two of us a perfect combination. Akira's blunt force attack was wearing me out, my shoulder muscles trembling from the effort to hold onto Tarik.

Neon blue fox-fire exploded around Akira, and I danced backwards warily. "You may control his sword, but not his fox-fire, which is the only true defense against mine."

Tarik vibrated rapidly, trying to communicate something to me. But what was it? "I don't have time to play twenty questions." It was then I realized with certainty that Tarik's emotions weren't affecting me, nor had he brought the magical armor with him. Was he weakened for some reason? Or something else entirely? Or maybe he was a bit overconfident like Prince Anyon had claimed.

Tarik swung through the air, taking my arms with him, plunging into Akira's fox-fire. His blade brightened to the same shade of neon blue, sucking away the fire, eating it like I'd seen him eat other flames before.

"No!" Akira bellowed. "That's not possible! How is he doing that?"

I grinned, the usual cockiness of Tarik's mood boost finally settling over me. "Tarik was forged in the flames of a phoenix." I wasn't sure if that was why Tarik seemed to enjoy eating flames, but what did I care? It sounded plausible ... and impressive.

Akira backed up a few steps, his eyes darting around as if looking for an escape route. "A rumor," he murmured to himself. "Just a rumor. It's an illusion. It has to be."

"Now," I padded forward slowly, placing one foot carefully in front of the other, keeping Tarik up in the air and ready, "tell me why you're really set on stealing Makoto for yourself. Maybe I'll let you live if you tell the truth." *But I won't let you keep those tails, which will cause your death. Oh, well. Too bad for you.* I studiously kept my gaze from the nine black tails, not wanting to give a tell on my intentions to remove them.

Akira swallowed audibly, obviously still shaken by

Tarik's fox-fire eating ability. "Makoto is a lost child of the Byakko clan. His immediate family was slaughtered when he was just a pup …"

I stilled, wanting and needing to know more. Makoto knew very little of his family. All he had were memories from when he was very young, most of them fuzzy, but he thought his entire family was murdered. He had memories of the massacre happening. When he'd first come to live at Domus Novem, he used to wake every night with nightmares, and he'd crawl into my bed so I could hold him. "What else?" I demanded. "What else do you know about Makoto's clan?"

"Even as a partial yako kitsune, Makoto would be welcomed back with open arms by his clan. I had hoped to be welcomed as Makoto's mate."

My muscles twitched, fatigue setting in from the battle. I wasn't in prime physical conditioning any longer, it seemed. "Partial yako kitsune?"

He snorted, backing up farther. "You know nothing about kitsunes. And surprisingly, Makoto lacks much knowledge, too. Or maybe not, since he came to live amongst witches so young. He has three white tails, even if the rest are black, he'll still … have purity within him. He'll never fully be yako. He'll never be fully dark."

"I don't understand."

"A yako must be born that way or made when just a pup, like I was, to ever fully be yako. Makoto will never fully be yako, and therefore he won't be fully shunned."

Relief flooded my system, and I grinned. "Good to

know. Thanks for that. Speaking of tails," I lunged, slicing wildly at Akira's backside, "I hope you're not too terribly attached to yours." My foot slipped, causing a misstep, and Tarik went wide, missing my marks. I growled in frustration.

Akira swung his katana, fury giving him a renewed fight. "My tails? You dare try to steal my tails?"

"Nothing personal." I sliced Tarik at his tails again. "I just need to borrow—all of them."

Akira snapped his fingers.

"Rems, what are you doing?"

My heart thudded loudly in my chest at the sound of Makoto's voice. My eyes darted to the side, not quite getting a lock on him. "Not now. I'm busy trying to collect some tails."

Akira took advantage of my distraction, maneuvering so my back was to the wall, and he was no longer cornered. He flashed me a feral grin, obviously thinking he was going to slip out the door and disappear. But I had other ideas.

"Barrier!" I yelled, hurling the spell past the kitsune at the door. He froze in place, realizing that I'd locked him in the room.

His lips curled into a sneer, long fangs glinting in the light as he snapped his fingers again.

"Re—" Makoto's voice choked off, followed by a gurgling sound. I whipped my head around. Makoto was staggering towards me, gripping a golden collar that was tightening around his neck.

"Let me leave and I'll stop it." Akira tilted his head, watching as if fascinated by Makoto gasping for air. "I still wish to make him mine in the future. I really don't want to be forced to kill him."

"You can't kill a kitsune that way!" I wasn't sure if I believed it or was trying to convince myself. I couldn't let Akira go, but I couldn't let anything happen to Makoto.

"Can't you? Like I've already stated, it seems the both of you know little about kitsunes, as shown by the lack of knowledge about what Makoto's become. So how about we wait and see what happens to him?"

I dashed over to Makoto. "I've got this. I've got it, do you hear me? You'll be fine. I'm here. I'm here."

Makoto's panicked black eyes met mine as he clawed at the collar, leaving bloody scrapes on his neck. His mouth gaped as he struggled fruitlessly for air. I lifted Tarik up to slice—

"Did I mention that the collar gives me control over Makoto? Very old magic. He can't call his fox-fire—can't use any of his gifts. In fact, it's sucking him dry as we speak, although slowly. And if you remove the collar, it will eat up all of his magic in an instant, killing him. So sad. But if I remove it, he'll be fine. Your choice."

Shit. Shit. Shit. Once again I was between a rock and a hard spot. I couldn't risk it, and either Akira had chosen the perfect bluff, or it was true. "Remove it now, and I'll let you go."

"Done." Akira snapped his fingers and the collar fell harmlessly from Makoto, hitting the floor with a thud disproportionate to the size and weight of the golden length.

I waved my hand, removing my spell, knowing if I reneged on the bargain that it would come back on me magically. The small agreement hadn't been hashed out with specific language, which in a way made it worse. "Go." I stalked forward, Tarik dragging low beside me. "Go before I gut you."

Akira didn't need to be told twice. With a parting glance filled with yearning directed at Makoto, Akira was gone in a whirl of tails and fox fur.

Tarik dropped from my grasp, disappearing before hitting the ground, and I rushed Makoto again, flinging my arms around him. I buried my face in his bare chest, inhaling his spicy scent. A trace of Akira's magic lingered, leaving a bitter taste on my tongue, and the desire to scrub the top layer of Makoto's skin off.

I hated that he'd been so vulnerable because of me, yet again. If I hadn't owed multiple favors to the smoke demon then Kiernan would never have been able to take me, and then Akira wouldn't have had the opening. Makoto could have been killed. As it was, I didn't know how much he'd been abused ... so much could have happened against his will. *Why was he under a sleeping spell? Why had they both been naked? What had Akira been trying to do, and how much of it had been accomplished?*

I dug my fingers into Makoto's lithely muscled back. "Are you—are you okay?"

Makoto threaded his hands in my hair, sighing heavily.

"I didn't trust Akira from the second he sauntered into this place looking for me." His grip tightened. "But I thought I could handle it."

"What did Akira do to you?" I trembled, considering some of the possibilities again.

"She used her female side in an attempt to seduce my male side. When I didn't bite, she tried to force me to change into my female side, I'm guessing so she could overpower me with her male side. But I wouldn't shift."

Rage boiled within me, making it difficult to say the words. "She—he was going to rape you."

Ignoring what I'd just said, Makoto continued, "She somehow managed to get that collar on me. I'm not even sure how anymore. It's kind of a blur … and was going to force my change by binding my will to hers. I fought even that—but then I guess she knocked me out." He pressed into me, a fine shudder running up his body, obviously as he also considered what could have happened.

I hated to ask, but I had to know. "What would have happened—what would have been the result if he had forced his male form on your female form?"

Makoto pulled me into him tighter, his breath warming the top of my head. "I can only tell you what Akira hoped. Both parts of that kitsune seemed to think that if either part of me was with either of its sides, it could bond with me." He tugged me away from him, his eyes bleeding from black to gold. "It never would have happened, Rems. My heart is so filled with you, there'd never be any room for anyone else."

"What about you?" His eyes darted back and forth between mine as he searched for answers within them. "Are you okay? Did Kiernan hurt you in any way?"

I shook my head, my throat suddenly tight. What Kiernan had done to me wasn't much more than harassment compared to what had happened with Akira. "No," I rasped. "But I met Akira at the Dark Court. Kiernan claimed to have summoned her. But I'm not so sure because of the collar. I think that kitsune has been watching you for some time, trying to figure out a way to get to you. It's all too convenient. And that pack of *Cu Siths* were focused on me. Probably commanded to get me out of the way. I think …" I nodded to myself, my intuition letting me know I was right. "I think Akira has been stalking you for some time, lying in wait for the perfect time to pounce. I'm pretty sure—"

Makoto's lips came crashing down on mine with ferocity, swallowing my words, blanking my mind. My body went boneless as I leaned into him.

Naked! Naked! Naked, my mind screamed. Makoto had never been completely naked in front of me before. Both parts of him had always been so careful to keep covered, much to my consternation. But now …

I slid my hands down his back, palming his bare ass. His skin was so smooth, like silk. Silk that I wanted to wrap myself in. He groaned, grinding against me. I gasped, biting down on his lower lip, heat uncoiling within me.

Makoto broke away from me, cupping my cheeks, our

little bursts of air intermingling. "Rems, gods, I want this so much—so much it hurts." His pupils were completely blown, the black only leaving a thin rim of gold. "But we can't here or now. I want our first time to be when I can claim you as my mate." He backed away a few steps, his eyes swirling with desire.

"I don't see a problem." I motioned to the bed. "We have that ... and a bit of privacy. Claim me now. Please." *Gods, please let him say yes. I can't wait any longer.* My body burned for Makoto, his touch the only thing that would be able to soothe me.

"It's not that simple. I want to do every part right." He backed away a few more steps.

My gaze dropped to his middle, my face flushing, my core becoming molten lava. "Makoto—"

"Right. I'm naked."

I blinked away purple spots, swallowing hard. The female version of Makoto stood in front of me, still very much naked. "Umm ... Makoto. You're still naked," I pointed at myself, "and I'm still bi-sexual."

She glanced down the line of her body, her cheeks flushing a delightful pink. "Oh! I meant to put my kimono on, not change."

"I think it was a kitsune version of a Freudian slip." I bit my lip, staring her down. "You don't want to stop, not really."

"Of course I don't," she growled. "I don't want to stop at all."

While she'd been talking I'd managed to close the scant

space between us. I grabbed her hair, yanking her head back forcefully, capturing her lips with mine. Truth was, I didn't care which side of Makoto I got to have first, as long I got all of her. Every single piece.

Makoto tried to speak, say something to chastise me, I could sense it, but I sucked her tongue into my mouth, eliciting a moan instead. I ran one hand up her outer thigh, lifting to hook her leg over my hip, opening her to me. All the while I backed her towards the bed.

"This I hadn't expected to find," Prince Anyon's sardonic tone sliced through my lust haze, and I whirled around to shield Makoto from his sight.

Makoto let out a squeak. "Get out!" she yelled.

A flash of purple sparked in the corner of my eye, and male Makoto, fully covered in his kimono, stalked towards Prince Anyon. "How long were you standing there?" he demanded, his eyes burning red.

"Long enough to see that Akira wasn't a problem after all." The prince swung his head around demonstratively. "Unless the three of you are having some kind of kinky kitsune party. And in that case, I want to watch." Crel appeared beside him, his jaw clenched and eyes glowing bright. "What?" Prince Anyon shrugged. "I said watch, not join. I'm still allowed to watch, aren't I?"

"Sometimes I think the *Anam Cara* bond hasn't affected you at all."

The prince swept his long fingers along Crel's jaw. "Unclench, my love. It would have merely been out of curiosity. Two kitsunes and a witch, even you can't claim to not be interested in how that would work."

"I'm only interested in you." Crel stalked away, clearly displeased with Prince Anyon.

"I love how possessive dragons are." Prince Anyon fanned himself, his eyes moving in the direction Crel had just disappeared to.

"Was there something you wanted?" Makoto demanded.

"I simply came to check on things, wondering how much bloodshed there'd be. Where is Akira anyway?"

I cursed under my breath, realizing how stupid I'd been to get caught up with Makoto with thoughts of sex, and bonding, and—I cursed again—I had to think about how the hell I was going to get nine yako tails before my time ran out.

Makoto snatched my wrist, running his thumb over the countdown tattoo. "What is this?" His gaze lifted to mine. "What is this, Rems?"

The prince glided forward, staring at the tattoo as well. "What new trouble has our dear little *cailleach* gotten herself into now? I would have thought you still had plenty to deal with from before."

I closed my eyes and exhaled, yanking my arm away from Makoto. "I did what I had to do to get away from Kiernan. But now—" I turned away from him. "Well, I kind of owe that shadow demon nine yako kitsune tails before this countdown runs out."

Makoto grabbed my shoulders, spinning me towards him. "Or what? What is the price for failure?"

"I'll owe him nine favors …" I swallowed around the lump in my throat. *It seemed like a good bargain at the time.*

"Nine favors?" Makoto's voice went up a few octaves. "Nine favors to a demon?" A string of expletives in Japanese exploded from Makoto, too fast for my rune to translate, not that I didn't get the gist of what he was saying.

"Why nine yako kitsune tails, pray tell?" Prince Anyon asked from his lounging position on the corner of the bed. "I thought you were confident in Makoto's faithfulness?" He lifted his brows, his eyes dancing with mirth.

"I trusted—trust Makoto. I simply didn't—don't trust Akira. And rightly so." I snagged the golden collar from the ground, waving it in the prince's face. "While you and Crel were getting down and dirty in the next room, Akira was attempting to—to—" I couldn't even say the words. I hurled the collar across the room. "So thanks for nothing, as usual, your highness." I turned back to Makoto. "I did what I had to do, just like I always."

Makoto hung his head as he tugged at the two braids at his temples. "I just wish you wouldn't have to. I should have been the one saving you. And now—you can't owe a demon nine favors. We have to do something."

Crel appeared at Prince Anyon's side. "Kiernan is preparing to march with his new army upon the Light Court."

Prince Anyon popped to his feet, his visage clouding over. "How do you know?"

"Because he's so confident of his success, he sent a missive letting us know of his plans."

"You're kidding?" I gnawed on my thumbnail. "He just told you to prepare to be conquered, or something like that?"

Crel gave me the side eye, stiffening. I recognized the body language. "Hey!" I said, hitting him in the arm. "What else? What else did that goblin asshat say?"

The Prince and Crel had a silent conversation before Crel said, "He wants you returned. If we hand you over, he'll leave the Light Court alone ... indefinitely."

Before I could even blink, Makoto was in front of me brandishing Tarik. "Don't even think about it," he snarled.

Prince Anyon raised his hands in the air, frustration marring his handsome features. "I thought we were past all of that. I've let you into my home. I've even let you insult me on numerous occasions with no recourse on my part. I've gone as far as—"

Crel pulled the prince into his side, kissing the top of his head. "What my *Anam Cara* is trying to communicate is ... He thinks of you as friends. And he would never betray his friends."

"Friends?" Makoto and I said in unison.

"Yes." Prince Anyon scowled, the expression bordering on petulant.

"And when did this happen? This change in status from lowly *cailleach* and her annoying kitsune to friends?

Because I seem to remember you claiming friendship before, and then you were hell-bent on punishing me for what happened with Crel. Even after I told you it was for Makoto."

Prince Anyon shrugged, turning his head, and acting every bit the spoiled fae brat I knew he was.

Crel answered for him, "When you told me that Anyon loved me. Plus, if he hadn't thought of you as a friend, then you'd be dead after what you did. Instead, he'd merely wanted to punish you."

"Oh. Oh!" I'd almost forgotten about that. After I'd faced off with Crel and taken the fae charm from him, I'd told him that Prince Anyon did love him and that he was just scared—that he shouldn't give up on him.

"Yes, those words, maybe insignificant to you, were what spurred me to truly give him another chance."

I grinned. "Want to thank me, your highness? Because something like that—getting you back your love—seems to deserve a thanks."

"No," he snapped. "I won't owe you an official favor, regardless of how I think of you now."

"Worth a try," Makoto whispered, sending Tarik away, and taking my hand.

"All right then. So I guess we need some sort of plan." And gods knew, I wouldn't be the one coming up with it, because lately all my brilliant ideas blew up in my face.

I glanced at my wrist, the numbers dwindling too fast.

Yep, so far I was batting zero. It was time to let someone else take a swing.

Chapter 19

"Are you sure about this?"

"Just do it already, Rems."

I inhaled deeply, letting out a long exhalation of breath in an attempt to center myself. It didn't work. "I just think we should talk about your involvement in all of this first. I don't think you've—"

Makoto snagged my hand with his, running his thumb over the inside of my wrist where the countdown number had dwindled to a mere few hundred minutes. "You need me here, and I wouldn't be anywhere else even if I thought you didn't."

"But your family ..." I swallowed around the lump in my throat, blinking into the grey night. We were in the forest behind the Domus Novem manor, a place grown and cultivated for spells like the one I was about to do. It offered privacy from prying human eyes, and the necessary nature surroundings to connect me with the energy of Mundi.

"You are my family. Some kitsunes that I've never met mean nothing to me."

"But that's why—"

"No." Makoto's sharp canines flashed in the dim lighting. "They don't matter. You are what matters to me."

"You say that now, but once we do this—there's no turning back."

Makoto was only one-fourth yako kitsune at this point, which according to Akira granted him some leeway when it came to being shunned by his family. If he helped me take Akira's tails, he'd be shunned by all kitsunes for the rest of his very long life. No exceptions. Any who aided him in the future would be shunned themselves, which was a powerful motivation.

"I know what the price is, Rems. And nothing is too high when it comes to saving you."

"But I could do this by myself."

"No, Akira's stronger than both of us individually. Only together can we overpower and get the tails you need."

I knew he was right; it was just that it gutted me knowing Makoto was going to lose something else because of me. Makoto had the chance to connect with a family he thought he'd lost forever. Sure, maybe they were distant relatives that he'd never met or even heard of, but they were still family—family that would never want anything to do with him if he helped me steal Akira's tails.

Makoto pulled me into his side, his breath hot against the side of my cheek. "Look, Rems, I know you're worried about what this is going to mean for me, and that I haven't thought it through, which is true, I haven't."

I opened my mouth to protest, but he pressed a finger to my lips, continuing, "I didn't need to think it through, that's what you need to understand. When it comes to you, there's never a choice." He brushed his lips against my cheek, eliciting a shiver. "I'd do anything for you."

My eyes slid shut on their own volition, and I brought a hand up to settle in Makoto's silky hair. "I know you love me … but I don't know why." Makoto and I had never been similar in personality traits. The only thing we'd really shared was a devotion to each other. How could a being that was so perfect love one that was so flawed? Or maybe that wasn't exactly true anymore. The two of us had changed drastically since my murder. Perhaps we'd grown together … maybe we weren't so different anymore. Maybe my grey soul, and Makoto's white soul had twined to form a new color, one that we both shared.

"The heart wants what the heart wants, and mine has always wanted you." He broke away from me, giving me a little shove. "Now do the damn spell so we can get back to the Light Court."

"Okay." Maybe it didn't matter why Makoto loved me, just that all of him did.

I stepped into the clearing, sinking to my knees. I dug my fingers into the ground, stirring up the scent of dirt. The energy, the pulse of nature itself, hummed into my fingertips, crawling up and through my body, mingling with my own magic. I squeezed my eyes shut, picturing Akira in my mind's eye. "I summon thee. I summon thee, Akira. I summon thee. I summon thee, Akira. I summon thee." I chanted the words softly, using them as another focusing aid. Although Akira wouldn't be coming to us, we'd be going to wherever the kitsune was. I was using my magic intermingled with the Earth's to track Akira. Once I got a lock, off we'd go to get me those nine tails.

An image of Akira, perched on a barstool in female form, flashed through my mind. I didn't have to know the coordinates, or even the name of the place where she was, I only had to feel her energy and connect with it just the way I had. It was an advanced spell, one that I wouldn't have had the confidence to do even a few days ago. But now, everything had changed.

"Makoto," I hissed. "I've got her."

Makoto pressed in behind me, resting his hands on my shoulders. "Then let's go get that bitch."

My lips curled up into a smile as I loosed the magic, hurtling us towards Akira. One moment we were in the forest, and the next, a few heartbeats later, we were in a dingy bar bathroom.

I hastily stood, glancing around at our surroundings, Makoto doing the same. There wasn't much to see. A few stalls, one with a missing door. One broken sink with a dirty mirror hanging over it. The pungent odor of human excrement permeated the air, and by Makoto's crinkled nose, he was even less fond of it than me with his heightened senses.

"I saw her on a barstool, this must be the bathroom," I said for an explanation when Makoto turned to me with raised eyebrows.

"Makes sense."

"What do we do about the humans?" I hadn't thought about that until … well, that very moment.

Makoto smirked, reaching for the door. "Ignore them."

I grabbed his arm, stilling him. "You can't be serious."

His indigo eyes swirled with mischief when they met mine. "Got a better plan?"

Ah, so here's a little taste of the yako side of him. It wasn't as obvious as when he'd first lost his spirit heart and had been fighting to control the new urges, but it was there. The old Makoto would have been more careful, less reckless. I also didn't have a problem with it. "Nope. Let's do this."

Makoto grinned, yanking the door open. I strode out behind him, my eyes immediately zeroing in on the bar. My senses crackled with the awareness of Akira. She was sitting at the bar, wearing jeans, a T-shirt, and boots, obviously trying to blend in with the humans. Her gaze lifted to mine, and then flicked to Makoto, before coming back to mine.

She lazily curled and uncurled her fingers from the drink she'd been nursing and stood. "And to what do I owe the pleasure?" She bowed ever so slightly.

Without a word, since apparently Akira was expecting

some kind of tête-à-tête first, I lobbed magic at her. The blue orbs slammed into her chest, knocking her off her feet. Several humans screamed, and the large male bartender produced a shotgun, pointing it right at me.

In a flash of purple, Makoto sailed through the air in fox form, tails whirling furiously, front paws batting the gun upwards just as it went off. Spinning, its four tails flattened the man, the gun clattering to the ground as Makoto used the bar to change trajectory for Akira.

"Tarik!" The katana popped into my hand, ever ready for battle, glowing like a thousand stars had settled into his blade. I dashed around the bar, raising Tarik above my head.

"No! You can't! Please!" Akira screamed, her tails splayed out behind her. Makoto was sitting on her chest, sharp claws poised at her neck.

"Roll her over," I commanded.

Makoto shifted back to his male form, forcing Akira onto her stomach, using his body weight to control her, along with fox-fire to contain her arms. I was surprised how easily she was subdued, being how powerful she was, and how inexperienced in so many ways I was ... and Makoto. I guess it just went to show how together we were always a force to be reckoned with.

"No!" she screamed again. "I'll die!"

"You should have thought about that before you tried to steal Makoto!" Until the words left my mouth, I'd been in denial about why I'd offered the demon Akira's tails. I'd told myself it was merely because there was nothing else I could think of to give a demon to free me. It was the truth and a lie rolled into one. It was the only thing I could think of because revenge had been eating away at my mind, consuming me.

As I looked down at Akira, held by Makoto and his magic, completely at our mercy, I wondered if I'd one day feel guilt for my actions. A flash of Makoto naked in bed with Akira skidded across my mind. *Nope. She asked for this. She should have known better than to mess with a witch like me.*

I grabbed several of Akira's tails, holding them taut by the tip, and sliced. Akira screamed, pure agony beating against my eardrums. Without pausing I proceeded to remove all nine tails, the task easier than I thought it would be, even with my hands slick with her blood.

When I was finished, Makoto stood, his kimono spattered with crimson. I had the sudden urge to magically clean him, not wanting to see any physical signs of what he'd helped me do. A kernel of dread bloomed within me, worry for Makoto's emotional state. After all, he'd just helped me steal the tails from another kitsune. I wished I'd never let him help—but he'd insisted, and—*No. He'll be fine. We'll be fine. We always are.*

Akira gasped, reaching for her tails as I scooped them up. The dark fur was matted with blood, my hands already sticky with it. Her dark eyes met mine with hatred, but no words came. She clawed at the ground, attempting to pull herself up. I stepped back, Makoto tugging me even farther away a moment later.

243

"I'm going to end her suffering," Makoto murmured. I could hear the pity in his voice, which I couldn't blame him for. It would be the same if I had helped steal another witch's magic. No matter who it was, there would be sympathy on some level, no matter how deep down. Which was why I was concerned about Makoto. Pity was a step away from shame and guilt, two emotions I wanted to spare him from.

"Do it," I rasped, even though Makoto hadn't asked me for permission. I only sought to let him know that I wanted it done as much as he did. Nothing good would come from letting Akira suffer for a few more minutes. Plus, maybe it would assuage, just a bit, Makoto's sense that he'd done something wrong. He could at least remind himself later that he didn't let Akira suffer.

Several spheres of fox-fire zoomed across the bar, slamming into Akira, igniting her immediately. Without her tails, which is where her magic was, she had absolutely no defenses. Her scream only lasted a moment, before she went completely limp, the fire beginning to dissolve her body. The pungent odor of burning hair and flesh mingled in my throat with the already retched smell of the bar. I swallowed back bile.

I turned, gazing up into Makoto's dark visage, watching as the flames burned in his eyes' reflection. "You okay?" I wanted to touch him, comfort him, knowing what we'd just done had been easier for me than him, despite his reassurances that it wasn't. But my arms were full of Akira's tails, the mass of them suddenly feeling twice as heavy than a few seconds ago.

"I will be."

Prince Anyon and Crel appeared behind Makoto, both of their gazes going to Akira's burning body, before flicking to me.

"We're here to help," Prince Anyon declared. "Completely out of the goodness of our hearts—although it was my idea."

Crel exhaled heavily. "I know what you're doing. It doesn't impress me at all to know you're helping simply to impress me."

Ignoring Crel, the prince moved towards us, stopping, seeming to think better of it. "Crel," he said. "You take care of whatever is left of that body, since you're so good with fire, and I'll erase all of it from the humans' minds."

I snorted. "What does it matter? I thought you said—"

"Ignore what I said outside that hospital. It's better if the vast majority of them remain ignorant to our existence."

"Just let him help," Crel grumbled. "He'll be insufferable if you don't."

As if he isn't already. I rolled my eyes but didn't feel like arguing with him, for once. Emotional exhaustion weighed heavily upon me. And I still had a demon to summon and a debt to pay.

"I'm going to go take care of the pesky demon problem. I'll be in the bathroom," I said, loud enough for everyone to hear.

Prince Anyon tilted his head. "The bathroom?"

"Go outside, Rems. That place is disgusting."

"Exactly. I thought it would suit the mood. Disgusting human bathroom for a meeting with a demon."

Despite everything, a smile tipped up one side of Makoto's mouth as he shook his head. "Just hurry. The clock is still ticking."

I scurried towards the bathroom, trying not to trip on Akira's tails. "You don't have to tell me twice."

Chapter 20

My clandestine meeting with the demon had been completely anti-climactic. I'd given him the tails, my debt paid in full, and the countdown had unceremoniously been removed from my wrist. But it was like that in the magic world—things rarely ended the way they did in human movies and books. Sometimes something seemingly insignificant ended up taking on a life of its own, and other times, something that felt like it would end the world, slipped into the night, disappearing like the sun at dusk.

Or maybe that's how it simply was for me since my world revolved around Makoto. No matter what else happened, it all sort of faded into the background, dull shadows in comparison to the bright colors Makoto splashed throughout my life. I moved through things, big or small, my destination always Makoto … my home. And as long as I eventually arrived there, nothing else mattered in the end.

I clomped across the white glittering floor, coming to a stop behind Makoto. His arms were folded over, his hands inside the ends of his kimono. His indigo eyes swirled, lost in thought. I watched him for a moment, appreciating his perfectly chiseled silhouette. Or maybe it wasn't perfect in the pure sense of the word, or only to me it was, since everything about both sides of Makoto was always exactly what I needed, even if it was simply candy for my eyes.

I turned to leave, wanting to give him the space he so obviously needed, when he spoke, "I don't feel different anymore. But I remember thinking that I was changing, and I know that … I know that my choices about some things are different than they would have been before."

I chewed on my lower lip, contemplating how to respond. "When your spirit heart was first stolen, you did things that … terrified me. Your moods swung so drastically that I was afraid I was going to lose you. "

"Like in the woods, after I killed those fae guards."

"Yes, when you decided it was time to finally take that last step, right then and there, whether I thought it was a good idea or not." I swallowed, the memory still fresh.

I continued to back up, slapping at his hands as he pawed at me with no restraint. "You're not acting like yourself. The real you wouldn't shrug off my fears."

His eyes narrowed, flashing red, before bleeding into black. "The real me?" He thumped a hand against his chest. "This is the real me." He snatched my wrist, yanking me into him. "Every part of me has always wanted you—so much it hurts." He wrapped his arms around me, his nails digging into my spine as he molded himself around me. His breath tickled my ear when he whispered, "I don't want to hurt anymore, Rems. I need you."

Makoto had changed since his spirit heart had been taken, and yet he was still Makoto; still my kitsune, still the love of my life.

I pushed those bad memories aside, focusing on the version of Makoto that stood in front of me. He was looking for answers and for a bit of comfort. I could feel his doubt moving within him. He was afraid that I wouldn't love what he'd become. He was terrified, despite the fact that he'd only done it to aid me, that I would think less of him because of what he'd done to Akira. Makoto had always been like my conscious, but now we were both wildcards.

But I'd changed, too. Neither of us was the same. Maybe instead of him being the good one and me the bad, we were each a mix of both now. Perhaps we grew together even more. Maybe we balanced each other out in every way possible, the pieces of us fitting together like they never had before.

I cleared my throat, laying my hand on Makoto's arm. "No matter what happens, there's nothing that could ever make me love you less. Whatever obstacles rise up in front of us, we'll climb them together, just like we always do."

"I'm part yako, Rems, and as I get more power, the

balance of light and dark within me will shift. I don't know what that'll mean for me—for us in the future."

I shrugged. "It means I might have to slap you around a bit to bring you back to sanity, but I can handle it. Our lives have never been easy, and that's okay."

His lips curled up on one side, his fingers sliding into my hair. "I don't know what I'd ever do without you."

"You'll never have to find out."

"I killed someone," he blurted. "An innocent human, to save you when you were murdered. It was the only way to summon Kiernan in Somniare. I used a blood sacrifice to draw his attention. And I didn't care. I killed and then I gave him my tail." He pulled me into his arms, enveloping me. "I couldn't stand the thought of being in this world without you."

Burying my face in his chest, I wrapped my arms around his waist. "What would you have done if you hadn't been able to save me?"

"I would have found a way. I don't care what I would have had to do—I would have found a way."

We stood there like that, for I'm not sure how long, simply holding each other, our hearts and minds dancing around dark things, when a throat cleared.

"Kiernan has begun marching from his lands." I lifted my head, meeting Crel's gaze. "Anyon requests your presence in the throne room."

"We'll be right there."

Crel nodded once, disappearing.

"I have all this magic and I can't poof myself in and out

of places like fae and dragons. I got gypped."

Makoto laughed. "You'll be able to do something similar when your magic strengthens."

"Yeah, yeah," I grumbled, slinking towards the door, hating the fact that I had to walk to the throne room.

Makoto grabbed my hand. "We don't have to do this, you know. We could," he snapped his fingers, "disappear. Lay low until all of this blows over."

"But will it ever blow over? And where would we go?"

"Somewhere, anywhere—the realms can all burn, as long as we have each other …"

"I wish it were that simple, but it's not. And we both know it. If we don't have allies, a place to stay, eventually, we'll be found … by someone. We have to help Prince Anyon defeat Kiernan and get that charm back. Once that's settled, then the Light Court can help me deal with my father. You know we won't be safe until both of them are wiped from the board."

Makoto hung his head, his white hair concealing his face. "I know all of that to be true, and yet," black eyes lifted to meet mine, "instinct keeps telling me to take you and run."

"Ignore it, and if you can't do that, then fight it. You can't let that fear control you."

I tugged free of Makoto and clomped across the white sparkling floor, my black beaten-up boots out of place in all the opulence. Makoto's soft tread sounded behind me a moment later, as he followed me, just like I knew he would.

Chapter 21

High above the Light Court lands, in a tower meant mainly for observation, or perhaps a lookout of some sort, was where Prince Anyon had positioned Makoto and me. The view was stunning, and even though I was in the tower for less than a pleasant reason, the majesty laid out before me stole my breath away. Purple skies served as a backdrop for colors painted across a surreal landscape. Colors, which didn't exist in Mundi, made up the animals that flitted into view from time to time. I'd heard once that if humans stared too long at such things in Alternum, without the magical protection of fae, their eyes would actually bleed. I believed it.

I finally tore my gaze away, focusing on the task at hand. From our standpoint in the tower, I could use magic, and be relatively protected and unseen, which left everyone, including me, agreeable to the situation.

Makoto had thought it would be best for me to stay hidden away completely, but I refused to let Kiernan make me cower. I'd feel better fighting for my own freedom. I could only imagine what kind of fresh torture would wait for me if Kiernan got his hands on me again. I refused to let him make me feel powerless, like in Somniare.

There was just one thing that kept niggling at the back of my mind. Why was Kiernan so dead set on tearing apart Makoto and me, and Prince Anyon and Crel? There was an obsessive quality to his actions that normally would speak of a jaded or scorned lover, but neither was true in Kiernan's case. For not the first time, I wondered if he'd just lost his mind in Somniare completely.

I shifted from foot to foot, knowing that I should probably rest until it was time for battle, but adrenaline and nerves kept me wired and on high alert. Makoto, on the other hand, was in fox form, curled up on the floor by my feet, snoring softly.

I rolled my eyes, wanting to laugh when Makoto jolted up, ears pricked forward. A flash of purple revealed Makoto in his male form, with Tarik in his hand, full armor in place.

"What do you sense?"

His eyes on the horizon, he grated, "They're coming."

I'd wondered how they would attack first, and many hypotheses had been made by Prince Anyon and other fae while in the Light Court throne room, but no concrete answers had been revealed. Some of the court had panicked when Prince Anyon finally revealed that their

Queen, his mother, had been murdered. Of course, he took the opportunity to blame Kiernan, and I couldn't decide if he actually believed it, or was merely using it as a political tool to get his warriors fired up with indignity. None of it mattered to me, as long as no one handed me over to Kiernan on a silver platter.

"Redcaps," Makoto murmured. "And ogres."

Sure enough, a hoard of Redcaps and ogres, two groups of fae that normally didn't mix well with others, even each other, came thundering across the lands, their war-cries sending chills up my spine.

The Redcaps were easy to recognize even at a distance because of what they wore on their heads. They all donned red caps, which is where their name came from. They dipped said caps in their murder victim's blood, and when the blood dried, if they didn't replenish by killing again, they would die themselves. *Talk about motivation to be a serial killer.* Even though their stature wasn't terribly large, their razor-sharp claws and teeth could rip almost anything to pieces. And they definitely didn't suffer any qualms about killing, which made them that much more terrifying. There'd be no falling upon mercy for one's life with a Redcap.

And then there were the ogres. Just like in human folklore, they were huge, hideous, manlike monsters that preferred to eat raw flesh, preferably human. They too seemed to lack a conscious, and most magical beings steered clear whenever possible.

It was obvious Kiernan had decided to send in the

thugs of his army first, not a completely unwise idea. I wondered how Prince Anyon would respond.

But I didn't get a chance to see what happened next, not when Kiernan himself appeared in the center of the tower. He wore clothes similar to the ones he'd worn in Somniare, what I'd come to think of as 'his look', black leather and a thick hood pulled up over his head, making it impossible to see his face.

"*Cailleach*," he purred. "I thought you would have made it more difficult for me to get to you. Did you forget I've tasted your blood?"

Shit. I had. With everything else that had been going on lately, I completely forgot that Kiernan, as a goblin, could track me anywhere for the rest of my life, since he'd tasted my blood in Somniare.

Makoto stepped in front of me, Tarik glowing a vibrant indigo. "Maybe not difficult to find her, but definitely difficult to take her."

But unless we killed Kiernan, or figured out what his motivations really were, there'd be nowhere for me to hide … ever. "Why? Why do you even care what happens to me?" It just didn't make sense. Kiernan had what he wanted—his body, his throne, a chance at a real life. Why was he obsessed with Makoto and me?

His gloved hands clenched. "I want what's mine, what was stolen from me."

"Whatever you think you're still owed, it has nothing to do with me."

"If I can't have what's mine, I'll take what's yours—and

what's Prince Anyon's. The fae and witch debt paid to me in heart's sorrow."

"What? What are you even talking about?"

"Enough talk," he hissed. "I don't have to answer to you."

A cloaked figure shimmered into existence next to Kiernan. "Ah, I see I'm just in the nick of time."

My jaw slackened as I stumbled backwards. That voice. It was one I could never forget, and would know instantly anywhere. It was one that had sung me lullabies when I was a child, had taught me my first spells with care, and had comforted me after Callie was brutally murdered. Or as I knew now, the male who I thought I could trust but had stolen my sister from me.

"Father." I couldn't hide the hatred I now felt for him.

"You know."

I glanced at Kiernan, who had thrown his hood back, and was staring with confusion at my father's cloaked figure. *Something's not right.* "I know you," he mumbled. "But from where?"

Shifting my gaze back to my father, I moved around to the side of Makoto, who let out a low growl of displeasure. "Yes, I know. I know what you did to Callie. And to think she—I—we trusted you!"

"I regret that Callie had to die, after all, she was my daughter, and if I could have taken her power another way, I would have. In the end, it saddens me that she died for nothing. But I needed—need her gift. The one that's now inside of you."

"You'll never get it. I'm not defenseless like Callie was." Blue flames erupted from my palms, racing up my arms. "And neither is Makoto, unlike Callie's sprite familiar was." Poor Dizka, the tiny creature's body had been discovered in a broken mess on the Novem grounds the same night of Callie's murder. She hadn't stood a chance against my father. But Makoto would.

"Kiernan, remember Tala," my father murmured, his tone cajoling.

Kiernan ground his teeth together, fisting his hair. "Tala—not Tala—I can't lose her. Gods," he sputtered, dropping to his knees.

My father loomed over him. "That's right. They took her from you. You deserve to have what's yours. And if you can't—make them pay. Make them all pay."

I sent out a sensing spell in an attempt to figure out what my father was doing to Kiernan. I got nothing. "Makoto?" I whispered, giving my kitsune the side-eye.

"I don't know either. But he's not controlling Kiernan with outright magic."

Which is why I sensed nothing. *So what is it? What's he doing?*

Kiernan wailed, the cry angst-ridden, ripping at my heart. "If I can't have her, then I'll make them pay. All of them." He jumped to his feet, his icy gaze narrowing in on me, a lazy smile curling his lips. "You won't get away from me this time, *cailleach*." He stalked forward, his own magic licking up his arms.

"He won't kill me," I muttered to Makoto. "Stay out of this."

"No, Rems—"

"Kill my father." I couldn't do it myself, no matter how much I hated him now. I knew when faced with it, I wouldn't be able to actually take his life, even though he deserved to die for all the things he'd done, and I'd never be safe until he no longer walked this mortal coil.

"Are you—"

"Yes, do it!" I had to protect Makoto and myself. There was no other way.

I loosed my magic, shooting flames at Kiernan, using no particular spell, hoping the blunt force would take him off guard. He raised his arms, throwing up a protective bubble.

"Aw, my little *cailleach*. Was it the gown? I promise not to put you in pink next time. How do you feel about yellow?" Several pulsating orbs shot my way.

Makoto slashed two out of the air with Tarik as he advanced on my father. The third and fourth I unwound and absorbed the power before they reached me. My spine straightened with the jolt of energy. "Mmm … thanks for that."

Kiernan showed his teeth. "You're stronger than you were even a day ago. How?"

Truth was, I didn't actually know, but I could feel my power growing within me, each moment my magic built upon itself, expanding its reach. I had a suspicion it was because I hadn't been bound to Domus Novem during the ascension ceremony, but I wasn't completely sure. I'd been taught that I needed my domos to temper and control my powers, and that I'd be the strongest and safest within a domos. I'd never questioned my teachings, but now I wasn't sure about anything I'd learned. Maybe it was the others in the domos who'd needed me and not the other way around.

"Wouldn't you like to know?"

Kiernan tilted his head, his gaze focusing on my middle, like he could see inside of me to my magic. And who knows, maybe he could in a way. "You didn't steal it from someone. It's yours. At least what's growing."

My attention was diverted for a second as Makoto sliced open my father's arm, causing him to hiss in pain. I wanted to yell at Makoto to make it quick, painless, not that my father deserved either.

Within that split second, a few heartbeats in time, Kiernan made his move, using my distraction to advance on me. I gasped out a startled breath to see him so close, his leather-clad hands biting into my upper arms.

"Just when I thought you were going to put up a real fight." He laughed, the sound twisting my gut. I spun, trying to break his hold, my gaze snagging on the horizon —the very empty horizon. *No redcaps or ogres. And no waging battle. What the hell?*

And then I was falling through time and space, stretching and shrinking to squeeze through the fabric of reality. I fought the pull from the tower to wherever

Kiernan was taking me, my brain scrambling with the effort.

I landed on my stomach, my limbs akimbo. I sucked in a ragged breath, the scent of flowers cloying. As soon as I gathered my wits, I was on my feet, fingers splayed, pulling on my magic.

Kiernan faced me, his expression blank. "Just give me what's mine, and I'll let you go."

"You keep saying that you want what's yours ... But what is that exactly? Tell me!" I'd witnessed what my father had said to Kiernan to set him off, and yet moments before that Kiernan had gazed at my father with confusion. *What the hell is going on? How can I fight something when I don't know what I'm dealing with?*

Kiernan dropped to his knees, his head thrown back in anguish. "Tala! My Tala!" He teetered, falling forward to his hands. "I can't—I can't go on without her! I have to get her back—no matter the consequences. I have to get her back!"

Magic bled from Kiernan, the golden dust rising above him, gathering and swirling. My eyes widened as a picture began to form, people and shapes moving around us, submerging us in some other reality. I gasped and then lost myself in the image, a story from some other time and place.

A large white wolf raced through the woods, ears pinned back and eyes wild. Behind it, two males followed, one with a bow and arrow, the other some kind of knife, the blade glinting in the sun.

"Please, stop! Leave her alone!" A very young version of my father stumbled after them, almost unrecognizable, blood oozing from his mouth and various other wounds.

A female appeared out of thin air beside my father, offering herself as support. My father staggered into her. "Please, you have to stop them. Tala ... you have to stop them from hurting Tala."

She hung her head, gripping my father's arm to keep him steady. "It's the law. She's rabid. She has to be put down."

"No! No! She's not! I swear it! Someone did this to her! Tala would never do such a thing."

"Sometimes familiars are driven crazy by a witch's magic for one reason or another. And with a werewolf—she can't be trusted. She needs to be put down."

My father shoved at the female, a surge of energy giving him strength. "I'll kill anyone, I don't care who it is, if they lay a hand on her."

He ran off into the woods, leaving the female on the ground. She gazed after him, shaking her head. "Stupid witch. You should have known they'd find a way to keep you in your place. It doesn't matter if she's rabid or not, the fae, and the witches they have in their pockets, will make sure none of us ever have any real power. We're all still slaves and no one sees it."

The scene scattered, revealing real-time, and Kiernan still on his knees in front of me in the field of wildflowers. My father now stood behind him, his dark eyes locked with mine. His ceremonial robe was sliced open in several places, but he didn't seem any worse for the wear.

"They killed her before I could reach them. Gutted my Tala like she was a wild beast and not the female I loved."

Shock rocked me, my mind rifling back to something Makoto had mentioned to me in passing when we were in Somniare.

"There was once a male witch who fell in love with his familiar, a female werewolf."

"A werewolf?" I interrupted. "But that's—"

"As rare as a kitsune familiar, I know." Makoto squeezed my hand briefly before dropping it. "This was before it was ... frowned upon to have relations with one's familiar. Of course, it was still rare because most familiars can't take human form."

I nodded. I knew that. My sister's familiar had been a sprite. The thing hadn't been more than four or five inches tall. Magical beings were always drawn to be familiars, but not all of them were created equal. Usually, they were just needed to help out with small things, like channeling magic, mixing potions, just being a companion, nothing major, most of the time.

"The witch and the werewolf formed a bond so tight that when she was killed, he went mad."

"Oh. And then I guess that's when the rule was made. Which isn't really a rule, it's more just a—"

"It's ingrained in every little witchling's mind that a relationship with their familiar is not acceptable because it keeps them safe, and the familiar, too. If we— If you would have — If we had that kind of relationship when you were murdered, for instance ..." His voice cracked and he paused to clear his throat. "If we had that kind of relationship when you were

murdered who knows what I would have been driven to do to save you."

My heart sped up. "What happened to the witch, the one who went mad?"

"He killed a lot of people—witches, werewolves, humans—all before disappearing, never to be seen or heard from again."

Groaning, I shook my head. "Oh great. You know he's going to pop up again eventually to do all kinds of heinous things. Probably has a whole villainous plot laid out that he's just waiting for the right time to put into action."

Makoto threw his head back and laughed, the sound lifting my spirits. "This isn't a badly scripted movie, Rems."

Or as it turned out, it was. Had I known on some level, my magical intuition picking up on things I didn't want to face? It seemed as if my time in Somniare had been one big reveal, even though I hadn't registered most of what I'd been shown by my subconscious.

I brought a shaky hand up to my throat. "You-you're the witch that fell in love with his werewolf familiar."

I jumped up, the fact that my father was here causing fear to constrict my chest. "Makoto!"

"Is fine."

"Why should I trust you?"

"Tala … Tala … Tala …" Kiernan groaned over and over, rocking back and forth.

My father grimaced, waving his hand in Kiernan's direction. "Because I understand what it's like. Do you think I didn't know what was blooming between you and the kitsune? Do you think we were all blind?"

"Why is Kiernan like that? He had nothing to do with Tala. Why ..." Everything went back to my father, or Tala, really. I could see that now. I just couldn't figure out how it all fit together exactly.

I wiped my sweaty palms down the front of my pants. "Why did you marry my mother, and have me and Callie? Did you love us at all?"

My father's dark eyes burned, torment rising in their depths. "I tried to move on. I cared about your mother, but no, I never quite loved her. That part of me was dead. I can see now that it was all an effort in futility."

"And what about us? Callie and me?"

He turned his head, staring at Kiernan. "When I had Callie and then you, those were the happiest days I'd had since Tala's death. But then ..."

"Tala, come back to me," Kiernan muttered, still rocking.

My father placed his hand on the top of Kiernan's head. "When I discovered, quite by accident, Callie's gift—a gift thought to have been wiped from witches ..." He lifted his gaze back to mine, trying to communicate it all silently.

"You couldn't let it go. You'd do anything to have Tala back. Even murder your own daughter." I wondered again why Callie hadn't destroyed her gift. Why give it to me? She'd claimed she didn't know how to destroy the magic, but there had to have been a way for her to figure it out. After all, she'd managed to do all the rest with seeming ease.

He nodded once, confirming. "Callie never told me where she hid her power, and so I took over a group of warlocks, organizing them—"

"You were searching for the necromancy gift." At least I knew my father didn't want to raise some kind of undead army like Callie had thought. Nope, he just wanted to bring back one murdered werewolf. Not that it mattered, he'd still stolen my sister's life from her—and her from me.

"Yes, I had hoped to find where Callie hid hers, but there was no certainty of that. For all I knew, she destroyed it completely. In the meantime, I used the warlocks under my control to search within other witches for the gift. If it had surfaced in Callie, it was bound to emerge somewhere else, eventually."

"You never sensed it within me." It wasn't a question. I knew the answer. He would have taken it from me just as he had tried to from Callie. "Until I loosed just a bit in Somniare when I brought Eve to life, awakening the gift within me." That was why the warlocks hadn't seemed that interested in me right away, but then suddenly they'd been hyper-focused. They'd claimed it was because of the magic Kiernan had gifted me, and then stolen, but even after I'd burned through the surplus, going back to normal levels, they'd seemed hell-bent on snagging me, stealing everything I had. "And while I was in Somniare, before you'd discovered I had Callie's gift, you sent your warlocks to Domus Novem, searching for it. If you would have found out sooner ..."

"The witches of Domus Novem would still be alive," he confirmed.

So had my mother sacrificed our entire domos just to save my life? Or had she seen no other way in the long run? Unless I summoned her again, I'd never know. Or was that true anymore? I could ... I'd been considering using necromancy to bring back my friends and family. *Maybe I haven't lost them. Maybe I can bring them all back.*

"Why didn't you come for me yourself in Somniare? Did you lose the taste for filicide?"

"As a matter of fact, I did. Killing Callie, although I wouldn't hesitate to do it again if I could possess her gift, ate me up with guilt. If you were to die, too, I didn't wish to deal with such a matter directly again."

I lifted my hands, palms up. "And yet here we are."

"Yes, here we are."

I needed to keep him talking long enough for me to think up a plan. So far it hadn't seemed difficult, plus I was going to make it out alive, and I wanted to know the answers to all of my questions. "But where does Kiernan fit into all of this?"

My father petted his head gently, something he'd once done to me when I'd been very little. "Poor ... kid. Kiernan wasn't just a resident of Somniare, he created it—it was a part of him. Somniare didn't exist before him."

Which finally explains his control over the laruas.

"When you nearly killed him, a part of his consciousness was too weak to keep me out. All of my grief for Tala ... infected him."

269

My knees buckled. That's why when Kiernan had come back after I'd sucked his magic dry, he'd seemed hyper-focused on hurting what was between Makoto and me, and ... taking what was his. He was confused, a part of him mourning the loss of a love he'd never experienced. What he'd kept saying about taking what was his, his need for revenge against fae and witches ... all of it came from my father. None of it was Kiernan.

"So you brought me here to kill me? Or—" Hope danced within me. "Are you going to bring us back with necromancy?"

My father's face softened, a ghost of the male I used to know. "I don't want you to die, Remy. I won't be able to bring you back, none of you except Tala. To bring such powerful beings back would take too much—too big of a sacrifice. But—I thought, maybe first you could try willing me the power, gift it to me just like Callie did to you. If I hadn't come here with the option of leaving you alive, I would have taken Makoto's life instead of merely escaping to come to you here. And I wouldn't have explained everything—trying to make you understand ..."

"Why didn't you get Callie to do that?" *If I can't bring back my friends and family, then what's the point of necromancy anyways? Maybe—no.*

"Because she refused. She claimed to have had a vision that made her see why she couldn't do it."

"How do you know Tala won't come back different— changed? If you need so much power, who's to say if you'll have enough to bring her back the way she should be?

What if she comes back as something … else?" *Like a friggin' flesh-eating werewolf zombie.* I shuddered at the thought.

My father smiled sadly. "I don't care how she comes back, just as long as she does."

Yeah, you'll change your mind once she's munching on your brains. I forced myself to stop thinking of zombies and other horrific horror movie-esque things.

Could I do it? Could I just give my father what he'd murdered Callie over? What he was willing to kill me over? Could I give it to him and walk away after everything he'd done? A part of me wanted to get rid of it, necromancy being an unknown power that honestly scared me a bit. The only reason I would have kept it would have been to bring back Domus Novem, but now I knew I couldn't. *So what's the point to holding on so tightly to something you don't even want? For spite? Revenge?*

Makoto had killed an innocent human just to find Kiernan in Somniare for a chance at saving me. Just a chance. He'd told me he would have done anything— anything at all to save me. And wouldn't I have done the same for Makoto? Haven't I?

Maybe in some twisted way I was just like my father. How did I know there were any lines I wouldn't cross when it came to keeping Makoto safe and in my life? Sometimes you don't know what you're willing to do, or not do, until you're actually faced with the situation.

I imagined my sister's smiling face, framed by the eyes of a child, and how much larger than life she was to me.

And then I played her murder over in my mind, something I'd witnessed just a few days ago. Could I kill Callie, or my mom, or even someone I knew really well to bring Makoto back to me? I didn't think so ... but I didn't know for sure. I would never know for sure. Or at least I hoped I never would.

"I'll try to give you the necromancy gift."

It was probably a big mistake—maybe even the biggest to date, which was saying a lot ... but I didn't know. I just didn't know how far I would go to bring Makoto back to me. I prayed I'd never have to find out like my father had about Tala.

"That's my girl. You always were my favorite."

Chapter 22

A smile spread across my father's face, akin to the sun bursting through a cloudy day, lightening his entire continence and shaving years off of his appearance. Witches aged slower than humans, and my father normally appeared to be in his late thirties to early forties, but something I'd never seen before sparked inside of him, making him seem more … alive.

I resented and understood him in equal parts.

He'd wanted to move on with my mother, to have a family, to love all of us, but he couldn't get past losing Tala. How many innocents had suffered because of my father? And what would happen if he ended up dead after Tala's brought back, or if she died again? Was my father planning on making Tala immortal, too? I knew he'd been adeptly practicing black magic and had the power. But immortal didn't translate to un-killable.

I stood, brushing grass and leaves from my black clothes. "And what about Kiernan, what am I supposed to do about him? I can't have him stalking me for the rest of his very long life. He's been relentlessly annoying already and it's only been a few days."

"He's here for a reason. He'll be the sacrifice."

"Sacrifice?" I hadn't seen that coming, which of course I should have, simply because that's just the way my life had been going lately. "Umm ..." I gnawed on my numb nail, and crinkled my nose. "Isn't the point of necromancy to just," I lifted my arms in the air, "I don't know, to just raise the body? Isn't that why you've been collecting power?"

My father laughed. "For the recently dead, or even if you want to raise a revenant, but not if you want to bring someone back completely. Blood magic is very closely related to necromancy, sometimes the two cross paths, so to speak."

I thought of how I'd used blood magic to bring myself back from Somniare. Had I used a touch of necromancy then and not known it? It seemed likely now knowing what I did.

"So you want me to will you the power and then you're going to sacrifice Kiernan?"

"Yes, exactly."

I tasted blood as I tore my nail down to the quick, wincing. My gaze roamed over Kiernan as he continued to rock back and forth, mumbling about Tala. He'd gotten the raw end of the deal since his birth. He'd been feared, and then imprisoned simply for existing. And now, when he maybe could have had a chance—finally—to have a second chance at his life, it was going to be stolen completely. I felt ... I felt sorry for Kiernan.

I squinted up at my father. I'd always tried to be honest with myself, even when it came to my darker side. Even though I locked away most of my tougher to deal with emotions and threw away the key, I still knew they were there, and I knew my own personal limitations. I'd been raised as a Novem, a domos of witches who weren't known for being anything but morally ambiguous, but I thought even we had lines we didn't cross.

My father had crossed all of those lines. Every single one. He'd betrayed his family, and his domos. He'd killed innocents. And who knew what other things he'd done that I didn't even know about. Giving him more power, and rewarding him for his treacheries—

Maybe ... maybe I can't give him what he wants after all.

I flicked my gaze back to Kiernan. He'd helped me in Somniare. I was the one who inadvertently made him the pathetic creature he now was. I had to fix it. I had to make things right. *Because everyone knows Karma is a bitch, and I don't want her coming after me with that bad mojo.*

"How do I give you the magic?" I slipped my hand behind my back, wiggling my fingers, willing Tarik to find me. I'd hesitated to call him before, but with both Kiernan and my father here with me, I was confident Makoto would be fine. "Do I just tell you that you can have it?" I took a few cautious steps forward, my gaze locked on my father's. "I don't want to lose any of my other magic." And time to convince him of my sincerity. "I also don't want to see you kill Kiernan. I want you to let me leave before you do that."

"Of course."

"And I don't want to ever see you again either. Do you understand that? Go live your life wherever you choose, but don't ever come looking for me again."

"I understand." The bastard had the nerve to look a tad crestfallen. What did he think was going to happen? Seriously? Clearly, he was completely off his rocker.

Tingles of magic warmed my palm as Tarik slowly appeared in my hand, tentatively, sensing his need to be stealthy. As soon as I could solidly grip him, confidence surged through me, which I tried to outwardly quell.

My father's eyes darkened, glittering with some unknown emotion. "I'm sorry it had to be this way. I wish I could have spared Callie ... and you. If it makes you feel better, I'll end Makoto, too. I wouldn't want the kitsune to live like I have all these years."

A bespelled jewel dagger shot from my father's hand, hurtling towards my chest, the energy of it burning through the air. I moved to dodge, knowing I'd be too slow with Tarik or my own magic, and I hoped I'd be hit somewhere that merely injured and not maimed me.

Eve, appearing out of nowhere, jumped into the air, knocking the blade to the ground with one of her pins, which she was swinging like a tiny sword. The dagger tumbled to the ground with a thud. My jaw dropped open, confusion and then righteous indignation surging through me. *And where the hell did Eve come from? I'd thought she was gone, for good.* "I said I was going to give you the magic, and you were going to kill me anyway? Great parenting, *Dad.* Father of the year right there. Even Darth Vader saved Luke in the end." But the truth was, I wasn't going to give the necromancy magic to him. Maybe he'd sensed that—maybe—*No. It doesn't matter.*

I didn't give my father any more time to try and weave sympathy with his words. My mind was made up, once and for all. I lunged forward, letting Tarik guide me with his glowing red blade straight to where I needed to be. "You don't deserve to have anyone's love!"

Flames shot up from my palms, racing along Tarik's blade as he plunged straight into my father's heart. He staggered back, his mouth open in a small O shape. My lips pulled back from my teeth as a snarl crept up my throat. I twisted Tarik once, yanked him out, and sliced my father's head clean off. I turned away before I heard the thud, followed by a second heavier one.

I hadn't thought I could do it, but somehow I'd found the strength. I shoved the feelings of grief and shame down into the place inside of me, the deep dark one that could destroy me if I let the things that lurked there out.

"You should burn the head and the body ... separately," Kiernan said, his icy eyes meeting mine, before flicking down to Eve, who was dancing back and forth in front of him brandishing one of her pins.

I jabbed Tarik into the ground, using him as support to lean forward. "Kiernan, are you ... is that—"

"My mind is clearer." He turned to stare at my father's body. "The moment you removed his head I could decipher what was mine and what was his." He gripped his temples and rubbed. "Although his thoughts are still in there. I still remember the feelings of loss, the memories— all of it. It's just now I can tell where he stops and I begin."

"Does that mean you're done—" He disappeared, just popped out of existence before I could even finish my question.

How friggin' rude. Although I guess it does answer my question in a way. He's definitely not obsessed about destroying my relationship with Makoto anymore or he wouldn't have just left me here all alone. Right?

A ball of fox-fire crashed into the ground beside me, burning flowers and filling the air with singed petals, the scent pleasant somehow. Makoto rose out of the flames in his male form, completely unscathed. I glanced around for Eve, but she was gone. *Did I imagine her?*

Releasing Tarik, I launched myself at Makoto. He swung me off the ground, burying his face in my neck. Neither one of us said anything for a few moments, both of us happy to revel in each other's company.

"Is it finally over?" I whispered, afraid if I said it too loud I might jinx something. Us witches were nothing if not consistently superstitious.

"I think ... I think so," Makoto answered in a hushed tone. "Kiernan's army was all an illusion. There was no battle, nor is there going to be one. Everything was an illusion. Kiernan hasn't been accepted as the king of the Dark Court. It was all a lie."

"But I was there. In the Dark Court. And so were you, Prince Anyon, and Crel. And I saw the dark fae. I saw … it was all so real. Why? Why would he do that?"

Makoto's grip tightened around me. "I guess, after all that time in Somniare, he's a bit broken. And in time, he may end up being their king, it is his right, but nothing is that instantaneous. He simply wanted it to be. Maybe even believed his own lies."

"W-we should help him. What was done to him— none of it was fair." Maybe it was because Kiernan had saved my life, or that some of his magic burned within me even to this day, but I guess, even after all he'd done, I had a bit of a soft spot for him, especially since finding out that most of the cruel things he'd done weren't completely his fault. *I guess I don't want revenge anymore. Huh.*

A low rumble started in Makoto's chest, growing into a deep growl. "Help him? I don't think so," he snarled. "If he wants to live, he'll stay far away from you, and me for that matter."

I pulled away from Makoto, glaring. "I'll do what I want. Don't forget that."

He grabbed my wrist, his canines sharpening into fangs, and his eyes sparking with red. "No. You're going to stay far away from him. Or I swear I'll gut him and burn him from the inside out, slowly, with my fox-fire." Four tails fanned out behind my kitsune, his beast, or yako side coming out to play.

I yanked away from him, the urge to yell, scream, and pick a fight riding me hard, but I contained those urges, knowing what I should—needed to do to calm my kitsune. I pulled him down to me, wrapping my arms around him. "You're not going to lose me. I promise." I moved my hands in small circles around his back, his muscles relaxing with each pass.

"I'm sorry. It's just—"

"Shhh … I know." And I did. Makoto was part yako kitsune now, and even though he'd never go completely dark, never become a true demon fox, a small part of him had changed and would never be the same. It didn't matter to me. I would always love every piece of my kitsune. I would simply have to manage his darker emotions from time to time, and learn to be more understanding, or at least learn the motivations for what set off the yako side.

As I held Makoto, my thoughts wandered. I wasn't sure what to do next. Since I'd been in Somniare, it'd been one thing after another, and sometimes I never thought it was going to end. I'd faced laruas, deadly nightmares, vengeful goblins, spiteful dragons, a crazed father … hell, the list would go on for a while. And just like that, with one fell swoop of Tarik's glowing blade, it'd all come to a close. Okay, maybe not quite, there were still some loose ends to tie up, but for all intents and purposes, I'd cut off the head of the problem … literally.

"We need to burn my father's body, and separately from the head. I don't want to risk him coming back to haunt us later like some bad movie villain." I swallowed, remembering something else that needed to be done. "And the charm—the fae charm. I saw it around my father's neck just before I—before I killed him. We need to get it back to Prince Anyon."

"Umm … Rems." Makoto tensed around me.

I whirled around, breaking his grasp, and expelled a long breath. "Gods, don't scare me like that, I thought you were going to say his body was missing or something."

Makoto raised his arm to point, his clawed hand shaking. "I think we need to run."

"What? Why?" My eyes widened as I took in what was on the horizon. Then I squinted, shaking my head. They were still there. "No, that's not possible. They can't exist outside of Somniare." A hoard of laruas, nothing but a dark swirling mass, rolled like fog towards us, blotting out the sun.

I pushed through the gut reaction that Makoto was obviously having. We weren't in Somniare anymore. *I'm not helpless here.* "Stop!" I commanded, infusing the word with power.

They kept coming.

I raised my arms, igniting my magic into flames, shooting two streams at the hoard, hoping to at least deter them from their current course towards us.

They kept coming.

Makoto rose up into the air, fox-fire blazing around him, orbs of it zooming across at the laruas.

They kept coming, completely unfazed by either of our attempts to fight them.

"Yeah, I think it's time to run." I whirled around, snatching the fae charm from my father's body, forcing myself not to register what my fingers touched. I dropped the chain around my neck, and ran, pumping my arms and legs as fast as they would go.

"Any ideas," I puffed out, my breathing labored. *Cardio was so much easier in Somniare.*

"I don't know how to fight them, Rems. They shouldn't even be here. And even with the charm nearby with its magic boost—yeah, I've got nothing."

Shit. I'm not going out like this. Especially after everything we've been through.

"Mama!" Eve shimmered into existence directly in front of us.

I didn't imagine her. I stumbled over my own feet, face planting, and getting a mouthful of flowers. I rolled over, Makoto yanking me up. It was then I noticed that Eve wasn't alone.

There was a female, not much older than me, with long white hair holding Eve's tiny hand. "Come with me if you want to live." She grinned, sniggering, "I've always wanted to say that."

Makoto snatched me into his side and took off running, my feet dragging through wildflowers as I tried to keep up.

"Hey! Come back!"

"Mama!"

I'd given up on Eve—pushed her from my thoughts and accepted that she was permanently gone, something created in this world as a tool for Kiernan. I'd thought I'd imagined her when she'd appeared in the field to block the dagger thrown by my father. Now she just showed up with some strange girl right when I needed her? *Maybe I'm imagining all of it.*

"Khol!" the girl shouted.

"Got them," a deep male voice rumbled far too close for my taste.

A large shadow loomed over us, and I whipped my head back just in time to see— "Dragon!" I screamed. But it was too late, the ginormous creature scooped us up in its talons, and then everything shifted. One moment we were in the field of flowers with laruas hot on our heels, and the next ... what appeared to be a well-maintained lawn of a castle.

The dragon let us slide from its talons gently, Makoto and I landing softly in the plush grass. The dragon's red scales shimmered in the sun as it flew off to the nearby woods, just as the girl and Eve appeared before us.

"Mama!" Eve rushed me, knocking me on my back as she plowed into my chest.

Makoto was on his feet, fox-fire in one hand, Tarik in the other. "Someone better start talking, now," he growled.

The girl grinned. "Yeah, sorry about that. Sometimes my visions aren't that clear and I had a hard time getting a lock on Eve here. Once I figured out exactly where she was, then her presence helped clear up my visions about you two." Her cheeks dimpled as she grinned again. "And then I may have interfered a bit."

"A bit? You borrowed Tarik, a sword that doesn't belong to you, in order to—"

"What?" Makoto sputtered. "How—you can't—Tarik? That's impossible. How could you have possibly borrowed him?"

As if Makoto hadn't said anything, she lifted her gaze to stare with unabashed lust at the large male strolling across the field towards us. Not that I could blame her. He was tall, well over six-foot-five, if I had to guess, and stacked. His muscles rippled with every step he took, even though he was fully clothed in jeans and a Henley shirt. His face was chiseled, framed by dark auburn hair, burnished by the setting sun.

The girl bit her lower lip, stifling a giggle. "Sometimes I still can't believe he's mine." Her golden eyes seemed to turn liquid as she tracked his every move.

"My little queen," the male dragon rumbled. "Thoughts on the task at hand." He slid a muscled arm around her waist, pulling her into his side.

She swallowed. "Right. Sorry. I swear I have the attention of a gnat when you're around."

He chuckled. "I'm always around." He kissed the top of her head with affection, his green eyes flicking between Makoto and me warily.

"Okay, so, as I'm sure you've already figured out, we're dragons. Hello." The girl waved, grinning again.

"Tarik? How did you call Tarik ... my Tarik, to you?" Makoto demanded, his attention still focused on getting the answer. Not that I wouldn't mind having it myself.

"Oh right." The girl flicked her gaze away. "I meddled a bit. Like I said. And don't feel betrayed ... Tarik only came because I showed him how it would help you. He did everything for the two of you. He loves the two of you very much. I just drained him a little a few times." She smiled. "But don't worry, I wasn't risking anything. I saw that him being weak wasn't going to be a problem after any of the times I used him. It was all part of my master plan."

And I finally had my answer as to why Tarik hadn't been bringing the magical armor with him—he'd been playing hooky with a dragon girl, doing gods knows what, and draining his energy. It hadn't been overconfidence like Prince Anyon had suggested and I'd strongly suspected. A wave of astonishment rolled through my mind coming from Makoto, as he obviously came to the same conclusion. *Yeah, I'm right there with you. It's a bit shocking.*

I tilted my head and narrowed my eyes, wondering exactly how old the dragon-girl was. She seemed a bit ... daft ... silly? A bit too human somehow? I couldn't quite put my finger on it. And what dragon faction was she from? I'd never heard of white dragons before. The male had called her his little queen. Was she something special among her kind? Like an actual queen, or was it merely a term of endearment?

"You see I get visions about ... well, a lot of things. I usually try not to get involved unless it comes down to saving our dimension or something along those lines. And shit just got real."

Makoto shifted, glancing at me with confusion. "What's this have to do with us?"

I pushed to my feet awkwardly, Eve's arms locked around my neck. "Who are you exactly? And why should we trust you?"

"Who I am doesn't really matter," the girl said. "What does is what's going to happen to our dimension. You see, I was raised in the human world and I don't want to see things get any worse than they are out there. My people, or the people I grew up with, their job is to protect our world from invaders from other dimensions. The nightmares are from our world, sort of, so they're never going to see it coming."

"Nightmares?" My mind immediately went to the laruas. My father had said Kiernan was Somniare, so if he was Somniare, what happened when he left?

"I can see it on your face. You know where I'm going with this."

I nodded. "Kiernan has to go back."

"No. Even if we could find him in time and force him back, he'd eventually escape again. He's one determined goblin. Plus, he needs to be out here, in reality. His power will be needed in another catastrophic world disaster. He will, in fact, end up saving the world. I'll make sure of it." She tittered. "I've come to find, there's always another of those on the horizon, a possible world-ending disaster. I hardly ever get peace. Good thing I was here for this potential apocalypse as well. You have no idea how much work it takes to be at the right place and time ... not to mention the headaches I get—"

"My little queen," Khol rumbled, his lips twisting with amusement.

She cleared her throat, her cheeks flushing. "In the meantime, living nightmares are wreaking havoc on humans, and other less powerful supernatural beings. I think you saw some of the results at the human hospital."

I ground my teeth together, remembering the slaughtered humans ... and the protection bubble Kiernan had created. "They followed us out of Somniare. And now that Kiernan isn't there anymore ... he knew this would happen eventually. He knew and he didn't care."

"Don't be too hard on him. He just wanted—"

"A second chance at a life, I know." I honestly couldn't blame Kiernan. I'd want the same and do whatever necessary to take it.

"Why are you telling us this?" Makoto demanded, his fox-fire dancing around him. "And you never answered— why should we trust anything you have to say?"

"You know you can trust me. Your intuition tells you so, or you wouldn't still be standing here. We all know it. And I'm telling you these things because you two are the only ones who can fix the problem. Well," she locked gazes with me, "you are the only ones, *technically*. I mean, there are a few others that *could* do it. But the outcome would be less than optimal for them. Not like for the two of you, because I know you and your kitsune are a package deal. Just like me and Khol."

She wiggled more into the large dragon shifter's side. "Sometimes the actions of someone not deemed special, someone small in the great expanse of the world, can make big ripples ... can make the difference needed." She motioned to Eve. "Like her. Bet you didn't know that without that doll, this whole dimension would have crumbled by now. Eve truly is a wondrous ... creation. Made by accident from a combination of your magic and necromancy, calling a part of a broken soul to bring life. She was an accident, and yet ..." Her golden eyes swirled, beginning to glow. "It's always the ones you don't expect it from that end up doing the most good."

She was right. My witchy intuition knew she spoke the truth. Even though I didn't know who she was, besides some dragon, I trusted her. But it didn't mean I had to just go along with her either. "That sounds poetic, and pretty and what have you ... but what exactly do you think I can actually do?"

And really ... Mundi would have crumbled without Eve? A part of a broken soul was within her? Did that mean she was well and truly alive? That the version of her Kiernan had sent was the same one I'd animated in Somniare? Maybe he'd simply had to recharge her magic to bring her back, which would make sense since Eve had 'died' giving her magic to me. Maybe the broken soul had clung to the doll, hoping ... waiting. Was that why her appearance had changed when she left Somniare, because she had a legitimate life-force, an actual soul? One that had been altered slightly with blood magic, just like mine had been? Did that also mean Kiernan had sacrificed an innocent life to send her to me? Or was it different because she didn't have a flesh-and-blood body? And what had Eve been doing when out of my sight? Apparently being a superhero voodoo doll. Hell, maybe she'd been with Tarik, the two of them saving the world.

I wanted to laugh ... at everything. My emotions teetered on the edge of hysterics.

"Kiernan's magic is needed to seal the nightmares back in Somniare, to put things back the way they belong. Magic that lives in you."

I blinked a few times, liking where the conversation was going less and less with each moment. "I have very little of his magic left. Just what he willed to me as I grew up since it's a part of me now, not what I stole. And how would I do that? Seal them back in?"

"I've looked at all the possibilities from every angle, and the only way everything will work, is if the two of you take his place ... in Somniare. That realm can't be allowed to collapse. It would mean the end of everything as we know it. Therefore, someone has to be there to maintain it ... permanently."

"Live there?" I squeaked. "You're definitely crazy if you think that's something I'd ever do. You're going to have to track down one of those other magical beings that you just alluded to. It may not be the perfect outcome you're looking for, but I'm not living in some other reality. This is my world. This is where I want to be."

The girl's expression softened, a knowing glint in her eyes. "I know what it is to sacrifice for the greater good. But trust me when I say, as long as you have the one you love with you—your other half—it'll all work out."

It was true. Kiernan had been alone for all those years, centuries of nothing but other creatures' dreams and nightmares to keep him company. He'd gone mad. Makoto and I would have each other. Did anything else really matter? We could live an eternity in each other's arms, doing whatever we pleased. Maybe ... It didn't sound all that bad after all. Plus, I'd be in control of things in Somniare, just as Kiernan had been. We wouldn't be in constant danger like before. Nothing would be like before. Makoto and I could create our very own paradise.

Makoto side-stepped towards me, Tarik and fox-fire still ready. "You can't actually be considering this, Rems. You can't—"

"I am." I threw my hands up in the air. "What do we have tying us here anymore? Domus Novem is gone, everyone dead—and I can't bring them back. Your family is lost to you as well. All that matters is that we're together. We can be together there."

"Rems, no. We—"

"You saw the laruas. We're not safe from them out here either. In there, in Somniare, I'll be able to control everything. It's the only place we'll truly be safe and able to be together."

"We can go anywhere we want. Do anything—"

"Do you really think after the remaining domos learn about what my father did that they're going to leave us alone? They won't let us be together, if they let me live at all when they find out about the necromancy gift." He started to speak but I raised my hand. "Sure, we can defend ourselves, live our life on the run, but eventually … eventually we could—would slip up. I don't want to live like that. I don't want to always be looking over my shoulder wondering if each moment is the last with you."

"If that's—are you sure? Because you know I'll follow you anywhere." He turned to me, letting go of his fox-fire and Tarik, his focus solely on me. "I just want a chance to build a life with you. To claim you for mine like I've always wanted—like you've wanted."

"And we can do that in Somniare." It was like all the puzzle pieces finally fit. Relief washed over me, causing me to feel strangely buoyant. *It's meant to be. This is what's been meant to happen all along. This is why my mother sacrificed Domus Novem for my life—this is why Callie did, too. This is why I had to have the necromancy gift. Callie had eluded to seeing more—something beyond us … If I hadn't created Eve, then Mundi would have crumbled. I know for sure necromancy had brought her to life now, even if the intricacies still escaped me. Everything was one huge butterfly effect beginning long before I was born. It all started with Kiernan and ends with me going to Somniare. Or maybe it was really just beginning—for me—for Makoto—for us.*

I reached out my hands, Makoto slipping his into mine. I laughed. "I guess I'm not morally ambiguous after all. I guess I do care about a few things other than myself, and you." My thoughts briefly wandered to Miles, the thought of him making me smile. He'd be happy to know that, in a way, his life had saved the world, too. Wherever he was, maybe he knew, or maybe he'd sensed it from the beginning, how important each little piece had been in the grand scheme of things.

Makoto pulled me into his arms, Eve letting out a squeak when she got caught between us. "I don't know about that. Whisking me off to Somniare to have me completely to yourself? Sounds pretty self-motivated to me. You're as selfish as always."

I grinned up at him. "You're right. I haven't changed at all."

I turned to the white-haired dragon girl. "So that's it? We just make a home in Somniare? Seal it up, keep the nightmares where they belong?"

Her golden eyes gleamed triumphantly. "You'll know what to do when you get there. I've seen it." She winked. "Oh, but—Oh! I almost forgot! I need the fae charm!"

I reluctantly handed it to her, dropping it in her outstretched hand, having almost forgotten about the thing in all of the excitement. Or maybe I kind of wanted to keep it. *Ha! There's no kind of about it! I would never say no to that kind of power boost.* "I was planning on—"

"Don't worry. I'm going to pay Prince Anyon and Crel a little visit … or I guess King Anyon now. Not just to return this," she dropped the silver chain around her neck, "but to let Crel know that not all of dragon-kind is unsupportive of his relationship. Plus, there's the little matter of who killed the Light Court queen. We have much to discuss."

Okay then, seems like she has everything well in hand, even if she is a bit … odd.

I was ready to begin my life with Makoto. I was ready to leave everything else behind—all the death, pain, suffering—everything except for my kitsune. I'd had enough of the real world.

We'd figure the rest out—plans for the future—after both sides of Makoto claimed me for a mate.

I was done waiting. So yeah, I guess I was as selfish as I'd always been.

"I'm ready, too." Makoto's hot breath tickled my ear, the tone of his voice warming my insides.

My mind flashed to images of Makoto and me naked, our limbs and bodies entangled—him on top of me, taking what he wanted, and her beneath me, writhing under my tongue. *Yeah, that all needs to happen. I need all of Makoto now.*

Closing my eyes, I willed us to Somniare.

Epilogue

Hate destroys. Love repairs.

Labels divide. Understanding unites.

There is no such thing as light or dark ... everything is grey.

Tenebris magic, lux magic ... one can't exist without the other. They are an ever-present yin and yang, serving as true balance, one unable to thrive without the other.

Gender is fluid because our souls are. Love is love, and can't be defined. Not that people haven't tried to do just that for millennia, and will continue to do so until we're all nothing more than fairytales written by rabbits.

Truth is, I don't know why any of us are brought into this mortal coil—what purpose we're supposed to fill between birth and death. Maybe everything is a wild card, and the best we can hope for is to have a few good hands.

I do know one thing though ... Whatever you believe or don't believe, don't overlook love. I know it sounds corny, but it's absolutely true. No matter who they are, find the other half of your soul and give them everything. Maybe that's the wrong answer, if there is such a thing, but it's the only one I've got. And really, I haven't been able to come up with a better one. I've been alive for centuries and peeked into an uncountable number of minds in the dream world, seen more than I ever thought I would, and love is the only thing that seems to mean anything ... at least long term.

"Rems," Makoto's voice crept along my mind, pulling me from my inner musings. *"We've got a breach. You coming?"*

Things hadn't gone exactly as planned in Somniare, but things rarely ever do. I'd learned that, too. Not that I'd ever been very good at making plans as it was.

I did finally get a life with my kitsune though. Both sides of Makoto had claimed me for a mate as soon as we'd arrived in Somniare. And to this day we still spend a lot of time, maybe too much time, strengthening our bond through a lot of naked time. *My life is so hard, I know.* When you're with the other part of you, the soul meant for you, you never get sick of them, and being with Makoto will never be anything but the happiest moments of my very long life.

However, we couldn't have children. A kitsune and a witch's genes aren't compatible apparently, which was okay with me. We had Eve, who was like a child who never quite grew up. Despite Makoto having hated her from day one, as it turned out, all because of an irrational fear of voodoo dolls, my kitsune had come to love her because I did. *Yeah, that's right, my big, bad, fox-fire wielding kitsune was afraid of voodoo dolls—thought they were creepy and bad luck. And I thought witches were superstitious.*

But if Eve ever turned out to not be enough, I could visit the dreams of countless children, of all species, any time I chose, chasing away their nightmares and becoming their imaginary, and yet very real hero.

"Rems, you coming, or what?" Ah, my ever impatient kitsune.

That was the other thing—although I had enough of Kiernan's magic in me to hold together Somniare and keep most of the nightmares where they should be, every once in a while, one slipped out into Mundi or Alternum. And it was our job to hunt down and kill whatever it was.

I'll admit, sometimes it was fun … okay, it was fun all of the time. I mean, what witch got to hunt nightmares with her kitsune by her side?

I'll give you a clue … just one.

I called Tarik to me, grinning when he vibrated happily in my hand, a deep shade of indigo. He enjoyed the hunts almost as much as I did.

"I'll be right there."

The real world hadn't seen the last of me …

And you probably won't either.

The End

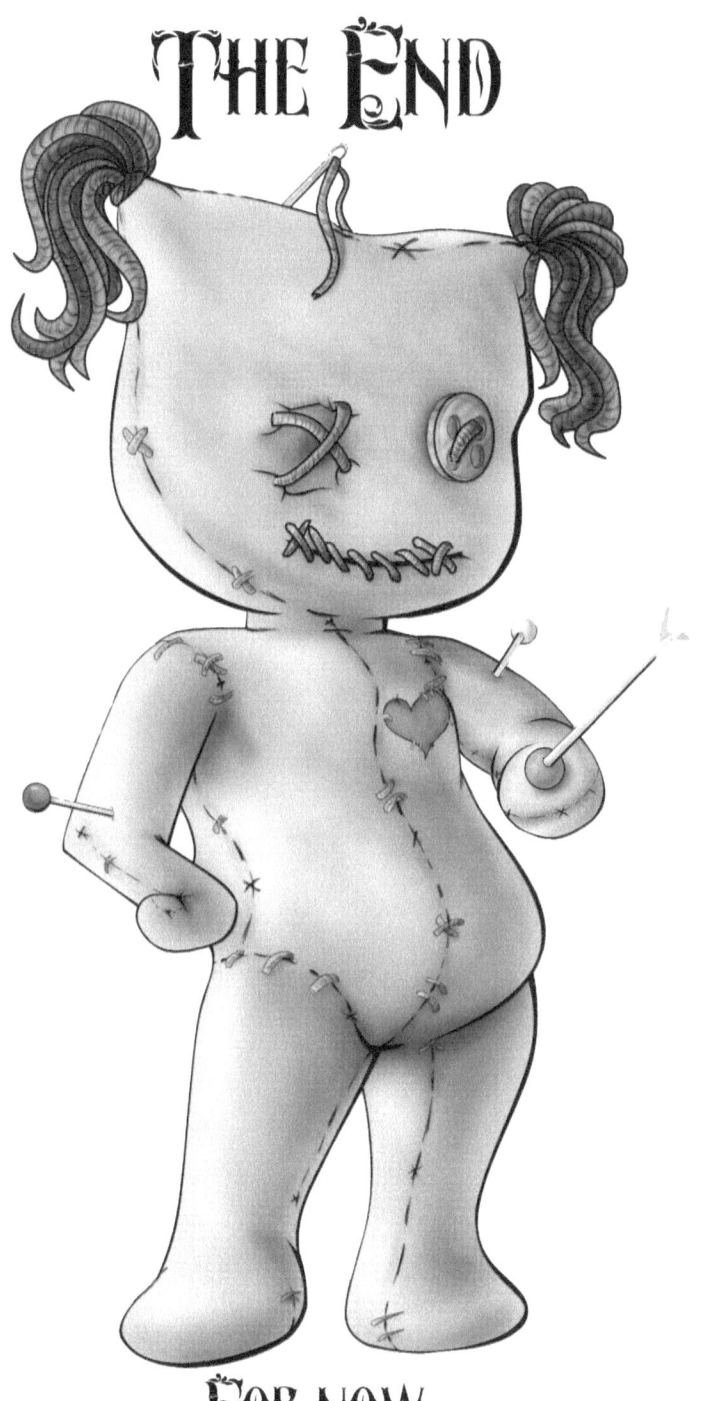

For now....

Acknowledgments

As an overthinker, acknowledgments are quite an arduous task for me. I wonder if I'm being lackluster or too intense with the thanks. Or did I forget someone? Possibly I gave too much credit to someone and therefore slighted someone else who actually did a ton. A part of me doesn't want to include these in my books at all because the people I appreciate should know it already ... or do they??? No matter how I look at it these damn acknowledgments make me friggin' sweat.

But here they are anyways since if I don't include them then people will probably think I'm ungrateful and weird. I mean, I am weird, but I don't want people to think that. I am grateful though, so I'll just go-ahead and make this uncomfortable for everyone. Heh.

Okay, here I go. Right now. Actual acknowledgments to follow. Hopefully, they represent an appropriate level of gratitude to all the people in my life that deserve it.

(And yep ... I have totally copy & pasted what comes next from my *Replayed* book acknowledgments, which I originally took from *Virtual Reality Bites* acknowledgments. I thought maybe after *Replayed* that I'd come up with something better. Or at least something new. Obviously not. So this is now copy & paste edition #9. Or 10? 11? Who even knows anymore. Therefore, I'm thinking you should probably get used to it.)

My amazing Hubby! Words can't begin to explain how supportive and truly amazing he is. Hmmm ... I think I already used the word amazing. But unlike in books, when honestly applied to someone, the word amazing means something, well, amazing. And my hubby is all of the things that word implies. Romance heroes are nothing compared to him.

Lindsay Tiry ... what would I do without you? I hope I never have to find out. From cover design to interior graphics to logos, you do it all. Your talent is awe-inspiring, and I hope one day everyone else will be able to appreciate how you shine.

Melissa Ringsted ... my illustrious editor. Without you, this book probably would have gone straight into the trash. Thank you for giving me the confidence to publish when I convinced myself that I was the worst writer in the history of writers, and for fixing all the words.

Ren, Kristin, Shona, Ruty ... my O.G. chicas ... I wouldn't be here without you. I'm beyond lucky to know all of you.

And last, but certainly not least, thank you to everyone who has taken the time to read this book. Hopefully, you enjoyed it, but even if you didn't, I still appreciate the fact that with so many options out there today, you even gave my book a fleeting chance.

About the Author

Ava Wixx escaped into books at a young age and decided to stay there. It was only a matter of time before she was driven to create her own fantasy worlds from fear of running out of places to explore.

Reader, writer, dreamer … Ava only toils in reality when absolutely necessary. She lives in North Carolina with her husband, and spoiled mini-poodle.

www.ingramcontent.com/pod-product-compliance
Lightning Source LLC
Chambersburg PA
CBHW020409260626
47156CB00007B/2307